"*Rufus is a delightful journey from conception to maturity of a humanoid loaded with AI.*"

—C. S.

"*In this latest book Welch has presented a look into what changes emerging robotic technologies will cause in our lives. We know that we are currently in the "Age of Alexia", and will undoubtedly soon find ourselves in the "Age of Rufus". This writing probes the impact this age will have on Religion, government, Society, and Lifestyles. Definitely should be on everyone's reading list.*"

—S. W. R., Newspaper Publisher, ret.

"*Rufus shows that even "Humanoid's" can delight or embarrass the adults around them.*"

—J. M.

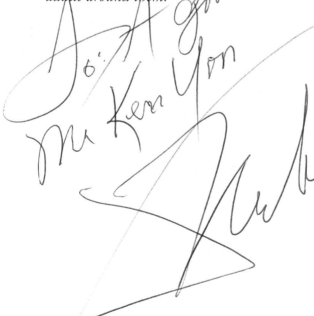

RUFUS I

J. ANDY WELCH

This is a work of fiction. Names, characters, business, events and incidents are the products of the author's imagination. Any resemblance to actual persons, living or dead, or actual events is purely coincidental.

ISBN 978-1-64184-629-5 (paperback)
ISBN 978-1-64184-630-1 (hardcover)
ISBN 978-1-64184-628-8 (ebook)

Let me tell you about a friend on mine. We've been friends since 2018. Rufus is an A. I. humanoid robot and is far more intelligent that any person. I've grown to a very close relationship with Rufus and all his amazing abilities. Quite frankly, I'll say the ole boy is a smart aleck hoot!

Rufus has no emotions. Yet, he imitates human emotions when it fits the situation.

Needless to say, I have gained a lot of respect for Rufus. One of his statements really stands out with me. Quite often he says, *"There is a Greater Being and humans need to pay attention."*

Rufus is characterized in this suspenseful book, "Rufus I". He's funny. He's serious. He's absolutely amazing. A renowned billiards player, world champion chess player, even a professional poker player wouldn't stand a chance against Rufus. In a courtroom, his legal mind will put the most powerful attorney at law to shame.

Rufus simplifies the greatest of feats as he answers human inquiries about America, politics, and the world, as he reveals where its' all heading. He carefully explains the solution for you and me.

My friend, Rufus comes to life in "Rufus I". I am certain you will enjoy Rufus and that he will impact your life as he has mine.

Rufus is busy these days as he works with me on the next series, "Rufus II"

TABLE OF CONTENTS

CHAPTER 1

Judy asks, "Carl, will you take Rachel's birthday card out to the mail box?"

"Okay. I'll pick up the newspaper while I'm there."

A clear early morning sky bares down as the sun is beginning to rise as Carl casually walks out to the road. Placing the card in the mail box, he reaches in the paper tray and retrieves the morning newspaper that was dropped off around five thirty a.m. Generally, he stops and listens for the birds chirping and singing and today is no different. The different birds singing seem to carry a nice tune, some nearby while others are distant.

Walking slowly back to the house Carl scans the headlines for any fresh local news, he notices a front-page article linking the same story to last night's local television news. And, the newspaper doesn't cover the television's early morning news. Over recent years, he has become less dependent on the local newspaper for up-to-date news. He watches local television news and is less dependent on the network's national news. His preference is to go online. That allows him to select the source, then to select the specific news article and eliminate their opinions. He wants to form his own opinion based on the best facts he can find.

Carl Forcrast and his wife Judy live in a quiet town in the northeast section of their state. Carl owns the areas' largest and most recognized jewelry store. Judy has been a stay-at-home mom for years and now three of their children are grown and on their own. The jewelry store has grown over the years to the stage of a full-time general manager and Carl is now in position to spend less time in the store and to enjoy the benefits of his labor in leisure.

"Carl, while you were outside, Fran called wanting to know what our plans were for the evening and invited us over for dinner. I told her we have plans this evening but, would like to visit. We tentatively set it up for another date. She is quite strange at times, but I like her. Ned is easy going and real nice."

Carl responds, "She talks too much and you can't get a word in at all. Then, when you do tell her anything of interest she doesn't seem to listen. She's already thinking about her response, an experience of hers that's bigger and better. However, I agree that both are good friends and we expect them to tolerate our short comings as we must also be tolerant."

Carl and Judy have been friends with Ned and Fran for more than 20 years. Ned sold his plumbing business and retired. Fran taught school for 21 years and then retired.

"Listen to this. The newspaper headlines read, *"Activists say locals are defying police orders."* "That is not true. It's an opinion of a few people that the paper's opinion supports! I'm not going to renew my newspaper subcription. They no longer publish the news, only opinions." says Carl.

"And, the same thing goes on with the news on television. Most all the news sources seem to go beyond reporting news with their opinions, most of which are twisted views. I now go online for news. I can select the news article I want to see and avoid the crap that is so opinionated!".

"Carl, they are simply reaching out for political and network ratings."

The jewelry store has a terrific staff and is, for the most part, on automatic pilot with daily operations. It's Carl and Judy's baby. They have grown the company from nothing to the success it now offers. Carl is readily available by phone and online to the store. He enjoys going to the store frequently, "just to make certain he still owns it".

"After yesterday's six o'clock news about those robots now available to purchase, I went online for more information. Those things are amazing! They're amazingly expensive also. Prices range from $22,995.00 up to and beyond $100,000.00, depending on what you want from them. As strange as it is, I'm interested in one."

"You want to spend twenty-three thousand for a robot?"

"No, probably over one hundred."

"Carl! No! That's crazy!"

"I understand your viewpoint but, you don't have all the facts. It's 8:40 am. Let's call that company and talk. I may change my mind. Or, you may become more toward the idea. Agree?"

"I guess. At least I'll listen."

Carl goes to his office at the end of their house and comes back with notes he has made, including their phone number.

"Come over here and sit beside me. I'll place the call on speaker so we can both hear."

Carl dials into the company. "Good morning, thank you for calling Lengra Robot Corporation, my name is Sarah, how may I direct your call?"

"I'm interested in discussing the purchase of a robot."

"Well thank you. May I have your name?"

"Carl Forcrast."

"Mr. Forcrast, I'm transferring you to Jodi Brasht. Please hold."

"Good morning, I'm Jodi. How may I be of assistance?"

"I'm Carl Forcrast and here with me is my wife, Judy. We would like more information on your robot, specifically your top-of-the-line model."

"Wonderful! That model R-016 is our humanoid robot. He is smart, of course and he interacts with people as if he were a human. He is amazing, absolutely amazing."

"Is there any warranty or guarantee?"

"Absolutely. The R-016 model has a lifetime warranty. Anything that needs LRC attention or service, even replacement as a result of any part or electronic malfunction is free of cost to you."

"Okay. What other details are available for us to reach a buying decision?

"Let me do this for you. Provide me with your electronic contact and I'll send you a video. It is about seventy minutes long and very informing. After you view the video, you may have a question or two, so call me at extension 1338. All contact information will be in the information you receive."

"That sounds good, Jodi. My email is C.Forcrast at CJJewelry. com. Can you send it right away?"

"Mr. Forcrast, it's on it's way as we speak. Is there anything else we can help you with now?"

"No. That's all. Thank you very much."

"We thank you for reaching out to LRC. I look forward to talking with you again."

Judy is still not sold on any purchase of a robot but she'll look at the video."

Carl goes to his email to open the electronic video from Jody. While he starts the program, Judy brews a fresh pot of coffee for them to sip on over the next hour or so.

"Okay, the video is ready."

"On my way, careful to not spill our coffee."

Both comfortably seated in front of Carl's computer, they begin to watch and listen. Carl stops the video along the presentation to make comments to Judy, explaining how he sees a robot fitting in to their life style. As the program ends, Carl saves the message for further review.

"Carl Forcrast, I can't believe I'm sitting here developing an interest in spending that much money for a darn smart hunk of wires, chips, and plastic. That thing is absolutely astonishing! But we don't need to spend that kind of money for a toy. And, that's all it is. It's a smart toy."

"That's not how I look at it. This R016 is like a person. Most people that purchase a LRC robot will avoid this model. Price will be one issue but most needs for a robot doesn't call for the advancement in R016. Even the five-year lease program is costly to some."

Silence as they think. Then Carl leans over to Judy, "You know me. Let's think about it overnight. Tomorrow, we'll talk. Agree?"

"Okay."

Judy walks into the kitchen, starts the coffee to brew as she thinks. "I still can't believe I am now becoming so excited about us owning a robot. That model is almost a hundred and fifty thousand dollars and we're seriously thinking about buying it?"

After some discussion over breakfast, they decide to call RNC after eating. If they obligate, and do not carry through with the purchase for any reason, they have been assured the deposit will be returned to them.

Still in the dining room, after their meal, Judy notes the time as eight-fifty. "What time does LRC open?"

"I believe they start their day at seven-thirty."

Carl takes a final sip of coffee and slides the near empty cup away. He takes a final moment to sum up their intent to obligate for such a purchase, then reaches for the phone and dials RNC's main contact number. The usual pleasant voice responds and connects him to a marketing specialist, "Jodi." Questions and answers stream back and forth between Carl, Judy, and Jodi until thirty-five minutes later, Carl offers their credit card and places a deposit on their own robot.

CHAPTER 2

Sunday afternoon, they pack enough clothes for a 5 day stay while in training. At 2:20 pm, Carl begins a three-hour drive to Lengra Robots Corporation, better known as "LRC". Very little conversation takes place during the drive as Judy is still thinking about owning a robot and, Carl is concentrating on driving. They arrive and check in at the Hilton hotel located near LRC.

Monday morning, they are up early, excited and ready for the meeting. Both are torn between excitement and curiosity. The drive through early morning traffic to LRC Is less than 10 minutes. They enter the LRC guest parking area and notice the facility of manufacturing and training is somewhat larger than anticipated. Hand in hand, they walk up to the front and up a few steps as Carl opens the door for Judy and they proceed across the lobby to a smiling face with full eye contact with them.

"Good morning, Welcome to LRC."

"And good morning to you. My name is Carl Forcrast and this is my wife Judy. We're here for training."

"Oh yes. Mr. and Mrs. Forcast. Your personal trainer for the week is Horace. He is looking forward to your arrival so; I'll alert him that you have arrived."

Within less than 2 minutes, a young man hurriedly walks toward them. "Mr. and Mrs. Forcast, I'm Horace Kringlare. It's my distinct pleasure meeting you both. You're in for an exciting few days. When did you arrive in town? How was your drive?"

"We came in last evening and stayed at the Hilton hotel. The drive was with normal traffic."

"Very good. If you're ready for the indoctrination, come with me."

"First we're going to the orientation room. This will provide you with some advance information about all aspects of the upcoming week."

The orientation room is more like a small auditorium with a seating area for about twenty-five people. Donuts, pastry assortments, coffee, water, and juice are available as Carl pours coffee for Judy and himself. They then select a seat near the front.

As more people arrive and it nears the scheduled meeting time, Carl estimates five couples in attendance.

At 8:00 sharp, a well-dressed lady approaches the podium located at the leadership area of the room. "Good morning everybody! And, of course you handsome Robots."

Carl and Judy turn to each other with the expressions, "Really? Robots among the audience? Where are they?

"Welcome to LRC. My name is Myra. This week may be one of the most exciting times you have ever experienced. After this orientation, you will be introduced to a robot stand. A robot stand is simply the appearance you select. After the selection, our lab will then bring your robot stand to life, so to speak. At that point, you will be formally introduced and will name your robot."

"A trainer has been assigned to you. Your trainer is always available to you at all times during this week."

"I'll now ask my assistants to come forward and hand out some materials to each of you. I'd like for you to meet my personal assistants. Here are robots Belon and Butler. Benson has been an assistant of mine since April. Butler came here from another department one month ago."

Judy and Carl are impressed, almost beyond reality, as they observe every move by the robots, their politeness, eye contact and movement, smoothness in their actions. In fact, Carl had anticipated some jerking movement as the robots move around.

"I'm certain that you want to know more about the creation of these intelligent robots. Synthetic artificial intelligence has been researched for years and with some ethical controversy about its manipulation of DNA. The process of replacing DNA software in a cell causes that cell to begin reading the new software. The first species disappear and the new species emerge. Artificial intelligence is a combination of computer science, physiology, and philosophy. The science focuses on the engagement of behaviors that humans consider intelligent. These robots can mimic human thought, understand speech and speak, and can engage in a game of chess with the world's most renowned chess playing champion and win every time. Do not play poker with your robot friend for money. You will lose."

"Our scientists are now able to understand and install neural networking in these computerized robots. However, robot neural networks are expressed mathematically. The great smell of perfume has to be expressed in numbers. In your robots' learning curve, they must catalog those numbers in memory so it will identify that smell next time. So, you will be guiding your robot to learn more senses that are being cataloged in their system. You will be encouraged to allow your robot to learn of your habits and expectations.

Carl, Markus, Janie, you have selected interest in the high-end, most intelligent, more humanoid style than of interest to another group coming in later this morning.

Through heuristics, the high-end robots are equipped with vast databases along with the ability to analyze and dissect problems. Their ability will therefore provide knowledge well beyond that of professionals of their field."

"These robots are the world's first completely soft, autonomous, and untethered robot. It is visually free of wires, batteries, and hard materials. It moves by pneumatic power; an internal-circuitry triggers chemical reactions, turning its liquid hydrogen peroxide fuel into a gas, which inflates the limbs and allows movement. Now, you may be comparing the robot intelligence to your personal computer, right? A high-end robot will provide you with more current and many times more information than your computer can possibly provide. How is that possible? These robots begin their knowledge from computerized input. However, at a point of advancing, they are programmed to search for other means of intelligence gathering, much of which is obtained from other highly intellectual properties. In other words, on their own, as they transfer out of human computers to other means of harvesting intelligence, and at super lightening speeds. They are truly amazing. The vast information they receive and process is beyond our comprehension as humans. And, they still have time to act similar to humans."

"One other topic before you meet your robot. In your materials that you'll take with you addresses the "Laws of Robots", and they are:

1. It may never injure a human being or, through their interaction, allow a human to be harmed,

2. It must obey the orders given it by their personal humans, owners, except where such orders conflict with the first law,

3. It must protect its own existence as long as the first law is not violated.

These three laws cannot be compromised."

"Conscience is a remarkable phenomenon that separates us from other forms of life. Your robot friend has no conscience, or as you Christians my identify, has no soul. It is totally void of emotions. That is important to keep in mind."

"While Belon and Butler are helping with the materials, we'll continue. Today, after an introduction to your own Robot, you'll name it. Then, you'll begin to interact and learn from it and, it will be learning from you. Just so you'll know, its intelligence level is very elevated when compared to your own brain power and, you may expect to ask any question, scientific, technical, or financial, as an example and expect an immediate correct answer. That is going to require an adjustment on your part because you may become alarmed and very defensive to have such intellect in your presence. However, that's okay. Welcome it. Enjoy its intelligence. Remember that intelligence is power."

"After this orientation, you will meet and name your personal robot, you will spend four days with your robot, night and day. We want you to be happy and comfortable with your new addition to the family. Friday morning is when you will make your final purchasing decision. Just so you will know, on the last day your robot can be re-programmed if you do not make the purchase or, even decide at the end of any day that you want another robot stand.

"Your personal trainer will go into great details about every aspect of training, owning, and enjoying your robot. By the training period end, you and your robot will leave here and travel back to its new home. If you are flying back home, you were advised earlier to purchase an extra ticket for your new family member."

"Now, if you have questions, your personal trainer will help you. My staff and I are also readily available for questions and assistance. You'll see us roaming around during the week. Benson, Butler and a few other robots that assist in training will all be dressed in navy blue jackets with the LRC logo on the back and chest area."

"If you will now stand, your personal trainer will direct you to a new friend, your robot. Thank you."

Horace walks up to Carl and Judy, smiling. "Are you ready for this big event?"

"You bet!"

Following Horace, they walk through an outer hallway alongside the assembly area. The left side of the hallway is all glass and they can view operations as they assemble robot stands.

Horace says, "We are currently building two robots daily and gearing up to build and ship twelve robots daily within a year.

We're receiving inquiries from other countries as they remain attentive and observant."

"I'm impressed." says Carl.

At the end of the assembly area, they enter a large room. Some others from the orientation are already there. Each buyer must wait their turn to view and select their robot. After about ten minutes Carl and Judy are led to an area with six different robot stands in place. Each robot is different in some way other than hair, color of eyes, and clothes.

"Take your time and select your robot. Keep in mind, your robot can have the outward appearance similar to man, or woman. Each has the same functions and only the appearance is different."

"Judy, what is your preference?" asks Carl.

"I don't know that it matters all that much. I do like blue eyes and short brown hair."

"Then would you like to select number four?" asks Horace.

"I don't know. What do you think, Judy?"

"I like number four."

"Let's do it!" responds Carl.

"Okay. In your email last week, you were asked to determine the name preference for your robot. What is the name you would like for your robot? And I need you to spell it, please."

"Judy and I want its name to be Rufus, spelled as R u f u s. Rufus Langel is the name of a dear friend of ours that passed away several years ago. Rufus was a retired professional singer in the rock and roll days."

"Got it." Horace reaches for his electronic devise and enters the selections. "Now, we'll go to your personal suite."

The walk down another corridor leads them to a tram system. "Your work suite number is seven. If you'll board this courier, we'll take the rail to your area."

The speed of the small rail courier is fast and within one minute they have arrived at their destination. Horace steps from the tram first. Carl exits and turns to reach for Judy's hand to stabilize her as she steps out.

Horace directs Carl to use his key card to swipe the entry pad. The door unlocks and Horace opens the door. Inside, the stylish two room suite is designed for comfort with a sofa, small table, 4 chairs, tv, microwave, huge bathroom, and a coffee maker and cooler for drinks. The bedroom area offers a king-sized bed with massage features.

"Oh, I like this. I only see one bed. Does our robot only stay with us during each day?"

"No Judy, Rufus will be with you twenty-four seven. Rufus is a robot. He may opt to become idle from time to time but he does not sleep as humans sleep. He seldom even purposefully rests."

"Oh."

All seated, Horace goes over some basic training details. "The nice thing is that you're going to enjoy the interaction with Rufus. I like to think of this week as continued orientation and just getting to know each other."

Horace reaches for and opens the small refrigerator door. "Judy, I'll bet you would like a soda. How about you, Carl."

"Water will be good." says Judy.

"Me too." says Carl.

"Before you came to our plant, we suggested you stay here at the facility as part of your ongoing orientation. We hope you'll find the suite acceptable and, if you need anything, my extension is 3110 or, you may call the main office at any time. The cafeteria is open from 6 am 'til 6 pm. We're all here to make your visit a pleasure."

"Thank you."

"One last thing, the television in your suite offers a special channel is dedicated to your new family addition. You may select channel 77 for more information about your robot."

"I'll leave you two alone now but, I remain available if you need me."

Carl and Judy look around the suite as they become familiar with the accommodations. The view out the large window offers scenes of nature as they are on the outskirts of the city.

Carl turns to channel 77 on the television. The overview of LRC facility and history goes on to how robots obtain their knowledge through new found worldly access. The presentation continues on to emphasize capabilities of robots and how they develop their new family traits. Robot owners are encouraged to refer to their robots as "he", or "she", and not as "it". The robot doesn't care but, your personal emotions to the robot develop stronger.

After the forty-five-minute presentation, Carl and Judy get ready, shower and turn in for the day. Once in bed, Carl is asleep within less than five minutes. Judy remains awake for over thirty minutes as she thinks about the day and anticipates tomorrow.

Tuesday is a new day for them. While enjoying a morning cup of coffee, Carl had already ordered their breakfasts that is being delivered from the cafeteria. The food presentation made it even more inviting as they ate.

Judy is brushing her teeth as there is a knock at the door. Carl opens the door to see a lady, dressed in the LRC attire.

"Good morning, my name is Cathryn and I wanted to make certain that you have everything you need."

"Everything is great."

"Please let any of us know if there is anything we can do for you during your stay at LRC."

"Well thank you Cathryn."

He closes the door and walks to the sofa to watch more television information about LRC and the robots.

Another knock at the door and Carl hears, "Good morning, this is Horace."

Carl opens the door. "Good morning Horace. Come on in."

Horace steps inside. "So, how was your evening at LRC. Did we fulfill your expectations?"

"Absolutely. Yes. I've traveled a lot over the years and have seldom experienced the exceptional service we've experienced here."

"LRC definitely strives to make this week very special for you both. The president of LRC is Mr. Claude Springfelt and he wants to meet you two. If you will, please follow me to the corporate offices and I will introduce you to Mr. Springfelt."

"Are you ready, Judy?"

"Sure. You lead the way."

Horace opens the door for Carl and Judy to go out as he orders the tram. It's about a three-minute ride to the LRC corporate office building. Arriving, the tram has actually traveled inside an area of the building and stops. Horace then opens a door and invites Carl and Judy to step out.

Inside a large room, a energetic, smiling receptionist greets. "Hello. You must Mr. and Mrs. Forcrast. My name is Ellen. Mr. Springfelt is looking forward to meeting you. Please make yourself comfortable and I'll tell Mr. Springfelt that you are here."

Carl looks for a magazine to glance through as Judy peers at all the paintings and items in the huge reception area.

Almost immediately. "Mr. Springfelt is ready. Just follow me please."

Ellen opens the door to Claude's office.

"Wow. Very impressive. Whispers Judy."

"Good morning Carl and Judy. I'm Claude Springfelt. Come in. Why don't you have a seat on the sofa? It's very comfortable. I'll get away from my desk and all its distractions and pull up a chair nearby. We are excited about your upcoming interactions with your robot, Rufus. Are our facilities comfortable for you?"

Judy responds. "Everything is perfect, absolutely perfect."

"I'm happy to hear that. I did want to meet you specifically, and I'll tell you why in a few minutes. Our research and development team has almost fully exceeded our expectations. Here's why I say that. Each robot is implanted, so to speak, with a pre-programmed system, a computer, if you will. We selected one implant to develop well beyond the normal implants. After we were satisfied with the design and internal testing of the "brain" as we may refer to it. Our R and D department refers to the development as XOP7. We believe XOP7 is ready for placement into a robot and field testing. Does all this make sense to you Carl and Judy?"

"Oh yes. I believe so. Says Carl"

"Now, you may want to know why I asked to meet with you, Carl and Judy. As we study and check out applications of all individuals that apply for each robot, it is important that LRC places a robot in a suitable environment. Our applications review department selected you as an ideal placement for this specific robot X0P7, as we know it. I understand that you named him Rufus. I have a very good friend by the name Rufus, a good name for your robot."

"Your robot is not only able to continually advance intellectually at a fast pace but, your Rufus is most intelligent. He is unbelievably advanced. A secret U.S. government agency has signed off for you to be the selected couple that will provide a nice haven for this particular robot. If all the plans come together in a few minutes your Rufus will become a great contribution to the United States of America."

"Now, you're going to meet a government agent that will answer some of your questions."

Claude goes to his desk and asks Catheryn to show the agent in. She opens the door to Claude's office and shows the man in, a young man probably in his late twenties, tall at about six feet, four inches, blond hair.

Claude then announces. "Carl and Judy, may I introduce Mr. Seth Buecrish. Seth, this is Carl Forecrast. And this is his lovely wife, Judy."

"Carl and Judy, today is a big day for not only you but, for the future of America. First of all, you both have been cleared for a high-level security clearance. You will have access to and be responsible for many upcoming things of a secret nature. You have been indoctrinated on certain aspects as to what and how these robots manage their intelligence and its expansion."

"Are you okay so far?

Carl responds. "Yes, we are."

"Good, I represent an agency in our federal government that has been working closely with LRC to design the one robot assigned for a special function. Your robot, Carl and Judy, is the only robot in existence with the special talents of which I am going to share a couple with you."

"Now let's dive into some capabilities that you may not expect. Your robot will be in frequent contact, indirectly, and consuming intelligence from a few selected satellites out in space. He will gain in general knowledge as it is gathering some high-level intelligence from the selected satellites and will immediately pass the information on the appropriate department. Your robot will not contact satellites directly. He will access information after it has been transmitted to ground units."

"Questions?"

"Wow! I don't believe so."

"Okay. You may now have some anxiety setting in. Do not worry about your robot. Rufus is very capable of handling himself in any trying and difficult situation that would normally cause you concerns toward its safety. He is very capable of handling himself in most any situation. So, don't worry. Please."

Claude tells Seth. "Just so you will know. Carl and Judy have already named their robot Rufus."

"Okay. Great. Thank you, Claude."

"Carl and Judy, you are now at a decision time. I have impacted you with some unusual, maybe even scary information and the responsibility associated with your robot, Rufus. What you are about to take on requires commitment. Are you ready for that commitment?"

Carl looks at Claude for a moment. "Mr. Springfelt, will it be okay if we step out for a discussion between the two of us?"

"Oh, absolutely. Take your time. If you would like, enjoy the comfort of our conference room to the right of Ellen's area. A phone is available if you would like to use it. After you are through, just tell Ellen and she'll get us back together. If you have any questions in the meantime, while discussing the matter, just let me know. You may dial my extension direct at star 1001."

"We'll do that. I'm sure we'll be back within ten to fifteen minutes, if that's okay with you."

"Take your time."

Carl and Judy walk slowly by Ellen's desk, smiling and nodding as they go toward the conference room. Carl closes the door and they set across from each other. The agreement consists of two pages that are to become an addendum to the original contract they studied back home. Carl begins on the first page and then hands it over to Judy for her to read. She tells Carl that she prefers he study the addendum and explain it to her. She knows he will pick up the phone and call Mr. David Lindsay, their attorney if he has any questions.

"Carl, what do you think?"

"The original contract had a confidentiality agreement within it. This addendum expands that language. I believe having David review the agreement would arrive at the same conclusion as us. It has severe penalties for any violation. We would need to pay out two hundred and fifty thousand dollars if we violate."

"That's scary. What if we slip up and tell something we shouldn't? What's in it for us? We go home with Rufus as a standard robot and with the original contract in place or, we go home with Rufus as a super robot and have this agreement hanging over our head?"

"Well, that's what we must decide now. We can go back and settle for their standard robot or, we can take this super intelligent robot home with us. They are no dummies here. They had a reason for selecting you and me. I guess it's somewhat exciting."

"Hmmmmm. So, what are you saying? You're leaning toward the super intelligent robot, aren't you?

"Well? Am I right?"

"Yep. Let's do it"

"It's your decision."

"No Judy! It's our decision, jointly our decision or, we don't do it!"

"But, you're the one comfortable with that contract that exposes us to a quarter of a million dollars. We'd have to mortgage our home and, it's paid for."

"Then we don't do it. You are either in agreement with me and we leave here jointly responsible in abiding with the agreement or we walk away from it. Look at me! Give me your answer now!"

Long pause.

"Carl, you know I trust your handling of our business and financial matters. So, I trust your inclination in this deal and I believe it will be more fun with a super intelligent robot over the ordinary intelligent robot that we came here to see. Let's sign it."

"Very well. The agreement requires witnesses to our signatures. Let's see if Ellen can round up a couple of witnesses."

Approaching Ellen at her desk and she says, "Well, that didn't take long. I'll alert Mr. Springfelt that you are ready."

"Ellen, first we need your help with the signing. The agreement requires two witnesses to our signatures."

"We can handle that." As she reaches for the phone and dials an extension.

"Cynthia, are you and one other person from your area available? We need two witnesses to a signing."

"Of course. We'll be right there."

"Thank you, Cynthia."

Ellen then dials Claude's extension. "Mr. and Mrs. Forcrast are about to sign the performance and confidentiality agreement. Cynthia and another from her office are on their way here to witness the signing. Would you like to join us and observe?"

"Allow me two minutes and I'll be there."

Claude walks out of his office bearing his normal pleasant smile. Cynthia and Randy from the accounting department approach Ellen's desk.

"Thank you, Cynthia. Thank you, Randy. Allow me to introduce Carl and Judy Forcrast. Mr. and Mrs. Forcrast will sign this agreement and, if you will, please sign as a witness to their signing."

"May I see your government issued identifications please? Says Cynthia.

Carl removes the driver license from his wallet and Judy takes a few extra seconds to locate hers, then she and Carl present them to Cynthia as proof of identity.

Carl and Judy sign three copies of the addendum and step aside. Cynthia then signs as a witness and Randy follows with his signature.

"Thank you, Cynthia and Randy." Ellen says.

Claude then signs each copy approving the addendum. He then attaches this agreement to the original agreement that has already been signed by all parties. One original is given to Seth, Carl and Judy a third original is retained as he hands it to Ellen for proper filing. He then takes two steps toward his office.

"Judy. Carl. Let's go back in my office. We'll discuss some details about the unique feature and capabilities of your robot."

Inside the office, Claude closes the door. "Why don't we sit at the small conference table across the room?

Carl pulls out a chair for Judy and she is seated. Then Carl sits.

Judy tells Claude. "I believe this is the most plush and comfortable chair I have ever sat in. And, the leather is so soft."

"Thank you, Judy. This table and the six chairs where a present from my wife, Gracie. I'll certainly tell her what you said. I believe they are imported from Italy. I agree with you. The chairs are comfortable."

"I believe you will be impressed with the extraordinary features and capabilities of your robot. You have selected the name of Rufus for your robot. I like the name Rufus. How you selected that name, may I ask?"

"Rufus was a friend of mine. He passed away several years with diabetic complications from a foot infection. Rufus, as a young man was a terrific entertainer and recorded several records back in the rock and roll era. He was the lead in entertainment at Las Vegas and other concerts that featured top name rock and roll entertainers. Our love and respect for Rufus led in naming it robot as such."

"That's a well-fitting name."

"Thank you."

"Your Rufus is truly a significant robot. It has an ability to connect direct and indirectly through other base units to some satellites above us. Rufus can access late minute events, even medical and political data that is unattainable to most. Beyond belief, he can quickly break some complicated passwords. Rufus has the ability and may use it to stay updated on legalities beyond most attorney's knowledge. A legal professor would learn from him. His medical knowledge can compare to that of some top medical scientists and doctors."

"These features are not that big of a deal you may say. So, let's proceed."

"There are hundreds of satellites of different countries orbiting our planet. His ability to indirectly gather information from a few and continually expand his own knowledge may be concerning to many foreign governments."

"Why is that, you may ask. As he expands his own capabilities, if the wrong people hear of those abilities, they will see Rufus as important to them, especially in spying on other electronics. In some cases, he may tap in to orbiting systems that monitor space vehicles traveling to or circling other planets and galaxies."

"Here are some concerns for Rufus in the future. Rufus will know details that are going on behind the scenes in high level secrets of governments and corporations here and abroad. However, you and I will not know. He is firmly programmed to not share certain information. Yet, he may use his knowledge to alert us of things we should do or prepare for as we move forward."

"Now, in the agreement is a clause that requires you to provide us with updates on a weekly basis. Updates of Rufus for the initial thirteen weeks and monthly thereafter. Your communications will be electronic. Instructions are in your packet that you will take with you."

"We ask you to be observant at all times. Rufus's capabilities are classified as top secret. Like most any other classified development, at some point, it seems to leak out to others that find a way to get their hands on it, specifically, in some cases, even enemies within our own country. You need to be watching for any odd behavior around Rufus. If you detect any strange behavior by any third party, you must call the phone number in your packet and report the activity. However, I will say that Rufus will detect any third-party behavior and react to it before you do."

"Any questions? At all?"

Carl looks at Judy. She nods her head. Carl responds. "No. I don't believe so at this point. We may have questions later on but, not now. We are taking on a lot of responsibility that I didn't anticipate, yet I look forward to our association with Rufus."

"That's why you were selected by the U. S. Government and by our company. Please feel free to ask any questions you may have while you're here and after you go back home. Carl and Judy, it has been a pleasure meeting and working with you. I know you will enjoy Rufus."

"It was our pleasure." Says Carl as they leave the office.

Seated on the sofa in Ellen's office is Horace. "You folks ready to go back to your suite?"

"We are ready. I didn't expect to see you here and waiting on us but, glad you are here."

"Did you enjoy your visit with Mr. Springfelt?"

"We did. He's very friendly, professional, straight to the point, and aggressive in a nice way." Says Carl.

Judy offers her viewpoint. "I agree. But, I'm scared of what we're taking on. This whole thing may become a nightmare!"

"I'm sorry but I'm not privileged to your visit with Mr. Springfelt and anything that may be of concern."

"Judy! That's enough! You and I will go through the packet and discuss the details once we arrive in our suite and become comfortable."

"Carl! Don't you become grumpy with me! I'm scared! You need to understand that!"

Silence as they travel through the facility.

"Carl and Judy. It's lunch time. Would you like to go by our cafeteria for a bite or, do you plan to eat in your suite?"

"What would you like to do, Judy?"

"Doesn't matter!"

"Let's take a detour to the cafeteria, and if you don't mind it may be good for Judy and me to sit at a table, just the two of us. It will be a good opportunity for us to go over our commitment so we both are comfortable with Rufus."

"Absolutely. That's a good idea, Carl. I'll grab a sandwich or something and stay out of your way.

You can just let me know when you are ready to leave for the suite."

Horace parks the vehicle and opens the cafeteria door for Judy and Carl. The fragrances of all the different menu items fill the room.

Carl says. "Wow! If you're not hungry when you walk in the door, you'll soon be starving."

Carl reaches for a tray and hands one to Judy. They walk slowly down the food line. Both reach for a salad and each knows what the other will probably enjoy. Carl pays the check at the end of the food line and they make their way to a table at the northwest corner of the room. It's secluded enough that the two of them can discuss their new undertaking.

"Hon, I see you got a pear salad. That's unusual for you, isn't it?"

"It is, I guess. I just wanted to change away from the normal vegetable salad."

"Are you okay with Rufus? You know that we can back out at any time. We can just tell LRC we've changed our mind. Or, we can deny the test super robot and go home with a normal one."

"No. I'm over my scare and concerns. I believe we have made a good decision that will lead to a great decision. I'm all in. As I always say, I trust our judgement as a team."

"Okay. Lets enjoy the lunch. We can go through the packet of materials later this afternoon.

I'm going to invite Horace on over. It's no use in him sitting by himself over there."

"Horace."

"Yes sir."

"Hey. Come on over here. Bring your food over and join us."

"Are you sure?"

"I am. Our discussion was brief. You're like family so, come on."

Back at the suite, Carl and Judy began discussing the responsibility they have taken on.

"Carl, I'm still concerned. I mean, our robot is different from what we thought we were coming to LRC for. From what I understand, if information leaks out about Rufus's abilities to the media or to spies, we could have a serious problem, even our lives can be in danger."

"Rufus is equipped to ward off any sharing of his capabilities and his information. If what you are concerned about takes place, and Rufus doesn't handle it, then we'll just handle the situation at the time."

"And the huge deposit we have already invested? What happens then?"

"We're covered. Within that investment is an insurance coverage that covers any loss of him, loss or damage of any property that he may be directly or indirectly involved, plus other coverage."

"I should have known you had everything handled and in order."

Carl opens the container provided by Mr. Springfelt. He first sees a thick manual, probably a hundred and thirty or more pages. He then spots a small flat box, red in color, appearing to be sealed and with special instructions across the top.

The secret appearing notices invites him to put aside the manual and check out the flat box.

"Judy, this appears to contain something of a confidential nature. Let's see what we have here. See if there is a knife in the top drawer beneath the coffee maker, please."

Judy locates a steak knife and hands it to Carl.

Before opening the box, Carl begins to read the warning message posted across the box top. "The contents herein are classified. A black box inside is only available for you to open. You must grasp the front of the lid while pressing down on the lid's back. The lid will then partially open. At that point, tilt the box slightly and a key card will slide out. Insert the key card into the two-inch slot on the right side. The black box will now open and ready to provide an important message to only you. When ready, remove the key card and your message will begin.

"Oh my gosh! Carl, this in becoming more and more scary to me. I'm going outside. I don't want to hear what that box has to say."

"No. Don't do that Judy. We'll be okay. I promise."

"I don't know. I guess I'll stay but, at any point I may leave the room if I don't like what I'm hearing."

"It's okay. I'm comfortable with everything and we're in no danger, now or ever."

Carl follows the instructions and sees the box lid open. He then removes the key card and hears a slight roaring sound coming from the box.

Finally, a human voice begins. "First of all the United States Government's CIA "Watch Dog Action Program" welcomes you and appreciates your volunteering. Please make no notes of the information you will hear on this devise. The message is only three minutes long and the message along with the devise will self-destruct at end. Let's begin. You must answer questions as we advance forward. On the box you see a green button labeled as "Yes". Another blue button is labeled "No". The third button is labeled "Stop". The stop button disables the devise and destroys all messaging. There is one set of listening aids in the box. Please put them on now. You will not be able to proceed and listen without this special listening aid. Press the green button when you are ready."

Carl turns to Judy. "Hon, I guess only one of us will be able to participate."

"You go ahead. I'm not up for it."

"Okay. I'll fill you in with the details after listening."

Carl positions the listening head piece. He then presses the green button to begin.

Judy quietly listens for any instructions that may overflow from the devise or Carl's ear attachment. All is quiet. She simply observes Carl's facial expressions for any notification of anything concerning or happy. He is showing no reaction. Three minutes seems like an hour as she waits.

In a few minutes, Carl removes the listening aid and places it in a small trash container nearby. He turns to Judy and is ready to provide an update. The devise content removal buzzing and clicking interrupts his discussion as it fulfills its final death wish. Carl tells Judy that he will discuss the details with her as soon as the devise stops.

After about sixty seconds Carl follows the instructions he listened to and places the entire box in a trash container.

"It's now dead."

"That three-minute message, for the most part, addressed the instructions and matters given to us by Mr. Springfelt. The instructions were very plain that we are on a secret mission and that Rufus will periodically upload certain data and information direct to the United States Government without us doing anything."

"Three minutes and that's all?

"That's about it."

"Carl Forcrast. You're holding back on something. I can tell when you're not being forthright with me. Now, come on. You had better open up to me right now!"

A knock at the door.

Carl reacts with "Come in."

The door opens and both Carl and Judy are stunned as their robot enters, "Hello, my name is Rufus, and your name is Judy? You're Carl"

"Yes, uh I, uh my name is Ju, Judy."

"I'm Carl."

Horace follows and closes the door behind him.

Rufus reaches out and shakes hands.

Carl is impressed with how the hand felt as he shook hands with Rufus. Rufus offered a firm but comfortable hand shake. Judy was tense and did not grip the hand at all. Rufus detected the softness of her touch and gripped accordingly. Rufus is standing with a ball cap on his head, dressed in a casual business-like long-sleeved shirt, khaki slacks, and walking shoes.

"May I sit?"

"Oh yes. Please sit wherever you like."

"Carl and Judy Forcrast. I know the state that you live in. In what city do you reside?"

Carl answers. "In a town called Commerce."

"Yes. Commerce. It is nice small town. Eleven thousand, hundred eighty-four people live there. The people are mostly female. The average income of people in your city earn forty-two thousand six hundred dollars and twenty-one cents per year."

Judy turns to Carl as she wonders how Rufus knew that much data, especially so quickly.

Then she looks toward Rufus. "Rufus that was a lot of information and very quick. Is that a normal expectation from you?"

"Yes. Rufus knows."

"I like you, Judy. I like you, Carl. I am happy. I hope you like me."

Horace sets back, quietly observing. "Rufus. I want to ask you some questions."

"Yes. And who are you?"

"My name is Horace. I work here at Lengar Robots Corporation."

"Now I know who you are, Horace."

"Rufus. Will you enjoy performing housework for Judy?"

"I do not know about housework. I will learn housework. I will perform housework perfectly."

"Rufus. Who was the 11th president of the United States?"

"The eleventh president of the United States of America was James K. Polk. Jim was born on November second, seventeen ninety-five in Pineville, North Carolina. Later, Jim lived in Columbia, Tennessee and he died in Nashville, Tennessee on June fifteenth eighteen forty-nine."

"Rufus. Do you know anything else about history?"

"Rufus knows history. Rufus knows answers to your questions."

"How do you know about history?"

"Rufus has many sources to capture and store information from."

"Rufus, you connect indirectly to a few satellite ground stations and their information, right?"

"Rufus will not answer that question. You may continue asking me questions of a different nature."

"Carl and Judy, feel free to ask any question of Rufus, of any topic."

Carl asks, "Is LRC a trustworthy company to do business with?"

"LRC is trustworthy."

"Rufus, from where do you obtain your vast knowledge? From computers?"

"No. Rufus is more knowledgeable than your computer. Rufus links and taps in to electronic data from most sources, sometimes the cloud information that provides quicker, more up to date, more thorough information than is available to humans and their home computers."

"Okay. I have another question for you. I have a MasterCard credit card in my wallet and access that bank online with my personal computer. Do you know my password assigned to that access?"

Rufus pauses three seconds. "You have two Mastercards. Which card are you referring to?"

"CitiBank card."

"Your password is P0o#3202W8I1 and you last accessed that account online at twelve forty-seven p.m. on Sunday."

"That's scary!"

Horace speaks up. "Not at all, Carl. Rufus has integrity and loyalty to you and Judy that is far beyond comprehension. Any information he knows or will know about you and Judy remains absolutely confidential and unshared."

"Rufus, are you ready to spend three days here with Carl and Judy to learn from them?"

"I am ready."

"Carl and Judy, how is your comfort level with spending the next three days with and learning about Rufus and his capabilities?"

"We're actually excited." says Carl.

"Okay. I'll leave you three alone now. Carl, you all just relax while you act and react as normally as possible through your interactions with Rufus."

"Horace. I have a question. If his power fails, the battery needs re-charging, what do we do?"

"Nothing. Rufus will know when his power needs attention. It runs up to 205 hours before recharging and it has many ways of servicing. Rufus knows and will always handle that task on his own. In extended outages, you are being shipped a solar panel for Rufus to us in his charging. You probably recall the panel description in your materials that will arrive at your home by Monday and will be delivered by overnight courier. You need not be concerned, ever. Rufus never sleeps. He never tires out and needs little to no rest."

"Understand?"

"Tonight and going forward, Rufus will simply sit, stand, lay, or whatever he elects to do, or is told to do while you rest. So, that may take some adjustments on your part as you become accustomed to knowing that Rufus may still be very active while you sleep."

"Now, I'll leave you all here to enjoy the rest of your day. I am immediately available to you by simply pressing this electronic button.

"Okay. Thank you very much." says Carl.

Now, alone in the suite with Rufus, Carl and Judy are noticeably uncomfortable in their attempts to strike up a conversation with Rufus.

Judy tells Carl, "I am very uncomfortable, even occasionally referring to Rufus as "it". I want to always refer to him as "he". Are you agreeable to that?"

"I sure am. I agree. Rufus is our friend. He is not an "it"."

Rufus speaks up. "I like that. I am happy to be your friend."

Carl looks at Rufus, "Rufus, you illustrate the ability to quickly respond with answers to questions that could take a long time for me to determine my own answer. Do you understand mathematics?"

"Yes. Rufus understands mathematics."

"Okay. What is 3,114 times .6 and divided by 63.2"

Quickly, Rufus responds "four point one seven rounded off. What else would you like to know, Carl?"

"Do you have the ability to share future individual stock prices?"

"I do."

"You're kidding! Okay, what will be the value of Sirius stock in one year from today?"

"There is a difference in value of stock and stock price. The value is not accurately predictable. Price is predictable only if I know who the person owning each share is and their patterns of buying and selling Sirius stocks. You must provide that information."

"But, how should I go about obtaining that information."

"You cannot."

"Rufus. Who will be the next president of the United States?"

"The candidate with the most votes."

The remainder of the following three days is spent with continued interactions with Rufus as the relationship flourishes. Rufus remains very cordial as he supplies answers to every question. By the end of their stay, both Carl and Judy are comfortable and very happy with their new friend, Rufus.

Friday, and there is a knock at the door.

Rufus asks "Who is it, please?"

"This is Horace."

"Come in Horace."

"I am assuming and it appears that you three are now quite comfortable with each other. I'll ask if you have any questions or any way that LRC can be of further service while you are here."

"No. We are anxious to introduce Rufus to our home. I sure hope he does not get car sick." says Carl with a hardy laugh.

Everybody laughs and Horace begins escorting them to the main facility and lobby. Rain is falling as they walk to their car and Rufus observes as Carl opens the door for Judy. Then, he opens the back door and Rufus awkwardly seats himself in the back seat. As they leave the area, Carl is reminded by the fuel warning system that he must buy gasoline soon. Within a couple of miles, they pull in to a convenience store and to the pumps.

Carl gets out, reaches for a credit card, scans the card, and begins to pump gasoline into the car. All this activity is being observed by Rufus from the back seat.

Both Judy and Rufus observe a lady walking from the store in the rain. She opens the back door and places three bags of purchases in the back seat. She then opens the front door, reaches in for her umbrella and is attempting to open it while standing in the rain. "She must be planning to go back inside the store. Judy tells Rufus." Finally, she opens the umbrella, positions it over her head to ward off the rain. Then, the lady opens her car door again, gets in the vehicle, reaches out and collapses the umbrella, places it inside the car and backs out of her parking spot.

"That was kinda' stupid.", Says Judy."

Rufus speaks up. "Not stupid. Strange, maybe. Not stupid. Her mind was focused on something else the entire time and she was not paying attention."

"Of course. I'm sorry. You're right Rufus."

Carl looks inside the car and sees that Rufus is speaking to him. Rufus then asks, "May I ask Judy to trade seats and allow me to be seated in the seat that is now occupied by her?"

"Ask her."

"Of course, you may. I'll trade seats with you until we are near our town at which time I'll want to return to the front seat."

Rufus gets out of the back seat, walks around and, as he has already seen Carl do, opened the right side back door for Judy.

"Hmmmm. I like you a lot already." says Judy.

Rufus then opens the door to seat himself in the front passenger seat.

Carl and Judy observe as Rufus places both hands on the seat and awkwardly twists his body to be seated then brings his legs inside. Both Carl and Judy giggle in a low tone. They are beginning to see certain movements and actions by Rufus as entertaining to them.

Carl completes the fill up and retrieves the card receipt from the pump, then sits in the driver seat. He writes the car's odometer mileage on the receipt folds it and places it in his shirt pocket.

CHAPTER 3

Their drive toward home is relatively quiet. Rufus is observing everything and everybody. He questions Carl about animals and farm equipment that he has never seen live before, although he has basic intelligence of their existence.

The time goes by fast as both Carl and Judy are busy observing and anticipating every action by Rufus.

They approach the city limits of Commerce and all seems quiet. The speed limit varies from 55 to 45 and then lowered to 35 miles per hour.

As he nears the 35 miles speed zone Rufus says "You should slow down now. There is a policeman ahead and he is monitoring all speeds."

"Thank you, Rufus. However, I'm not speeding."

Carl then sees the police car up ahead.

"He is going to stop your car." Says Rufus.

"I don't believe so. I am not breaking any law."

Carl passes by the parked police car positioned in a parking lot. Almost immediately he glances in the rear-view mirror as the police car enters the right lane behind his vehicle with lights flashing. Quickly, he realizes the policeman is signaling for him to pull over to the side of the road. He turned on his right turn signal and gently applies the brakes as he obeys the law.

Once on the shoulder of the road Carl opens the door to step outside. Suddenly, a speaker orders him, "Please stay in your car! Do not get out of your car."

"I told you" says Rufus.

"Knock it off Rufus!"

After the policeman runs his license plate number, he approaches the car. "I am corporal Buford Walsh. I clocked you speeding in the 35 mph zone. May I see your driver license, vehicle registration, and proof of insurance, please?"

Carl hands those three items to corporal Walsh and asks, "I was not speeding."

"We'll discuss the offense in a few minutes. Please remain in your car and I will be back in a few minutes.", then Walsh walks back to his police car.

"You're in trouble, big trouble says Rufus. I can help you."

"No Rufus! I want you to stay out of this!"

Carl watches through the mirror as he sees slight movement from time to time by Walsh. He turns to Judy and says "I have no idea why I've been pulled over."

"Hon, it will be okay. You were definitely not speeding. Just remain calm."

Rufus speaks up, "I know why."

Carl ignores Rufus and remains quiet as he waits for corporal Walsh to return. After another 2 minutes, Walsh gets out of his car, closes the door, and walks toward Carl with his ticket book in hand.

"Mr. Forcrast, I congratulate you on your driving record."

"I observed your vehicle as it appeared to be exceeding the limit. I then verified your speed on the radar speed measurement device that prompted me to pull you over. You were clocked at variable speeds that really do not make sense. I'm going to issue you a speeding ticket and a reckless driving ticket. While you were in the forty-five miles per hour zone, you accelerated very quickly to ninety-three and then as you entered the thirty-five miles per hour zone you quickly dropped to thirty-three and again sped back up to sixty-eight, then back to thirty-four. I really don't understand what you were attempting to do but, speeding is speeding and, your other violation will reflect reckless driving because of the extreme speed."

"Your driving record is free of any moving citations. Do you realize how dangerous your driving was to you and your family along with other vehicles? Why were you speeding so erratically?"

"Corporal Walsh, in no way did I exceed any posted speed limit. That I assure you."

"Mr. Forcrast, my radar equipment is fully certified and accurate within 3 miles per hour."

Rufus says, "I will handle this for you. I told you the officer would pull you over."

All of a sudden, Carl turns to Rufus "How did you know? Did you do something to cause this? What did you do?"

Carl then turns to the policeman, "Hold up on completing that ticket. There may be an explanation for all this confusion. Maybe both of us are right"

"I understand what you're trying to accomplish, but speeding is speeding and you were violating the law."

"Sir, I want you to meet Rufus. Rufus is a robot, one of the intelligent robots you may have heard or read about. With your permission, I would like for Rufus to get out of the car and explain everything."

"No! I want everybody to remain inside the car."

He leans over and addresses Rufus, "You have something to say to me?"

"Rufus likes you. Rufus has fun. Rufus relayed and altered the electronic signals back to your speed monitoring devise. Doing that was much fun."

The officer is startled and speechless. He has never encountered a robot before, never had a law-abiding citizen register speeds instantaneously jumping from 93 and back to 33, all while lawfully maintaining the speed limit.

"Mr. Forcrast, I don't know of a state statute that addresses such an incidence. You registered as speeding yet you say you were not. You have a robot that interfered with the law but, I don't know of any specific law applicable that I can charge a non-human with. I can let you go but, how do I explain voiding out a ticket at 93 miles per hour and reckless driving."

"Officer, I sure am sorry."

"Please remain in your car. I will return in a few minutes."

In the police car, Walsh contacts his supervisor, "Ben, I need your help on site at the 1600 block of Mays Rd."

"What's up, Buford?"

"I need to fill you in when you arrive. Basically, I don't know if I truly have an offense and if I do, I don't know how to write it up."

"Really? I'll be there in five."

Quietness lurks in Carl's vehicle as they wait for the next phase of the traffic stop.

All is quiet. Then, Carl sees another police car drive in behind Walsh's car. corporal Walsh walks back to the other car and talks to the deputy. Then, the two of them walk toward Carl's vehicle.

"Mr. Forcrast, this is Lieutenant Mills, my supervisor."

"Mr. Forcrast, why don't you step out of the car for me?"

"Sure."

"Now, tell me what happened and why you should not be issued multiple citations."

"My wife, Judy, Rufus, and I are driving back into Commerce from our trip to LRC and the purchase of our own robot, "Rufus". A mile or so back, Rufus told me that a policeman was going to pull me over. Of course, I paid no attention to the robot. Shortly thereafter, officer Walsh did pull me over and claimed I was speeding. At no point did I ever exceed the posted speed limit. Officer Walsh said he clocked me driving ninety something miles per hour in that forty-five mph speed zone and then, sixty something in a thirty five speed zone. He pulled me over and during the discussion we determined that our robot, Rufus caused me to be stopped. Rufus is an extremely intelligent robot and I believe he can explain everything."

Lieutenant Mills finds it awkward talking to a robot as he proceeds.

"Rufus? You caused a policeman to pull this vehicle over?"

"Rufus performs modifications in electronics, from a distance."

"I'm listening. Tell me more."

"Rufus can read and alter any nearby electronic device. Humans are incapable of understanding the process."

Lieutenant Mills is well trained at reading eye movement and facial expressions of people. He stares at Rufus for a few moments until he realizes that Rufus has no such expressions.

"Rufus, your prank could have caused Mr. Forcrast to be in serious trouble. He could have been taken to jail. I want your absolute assurance that you will never even attempt to alter police electronic devises again. Agree?"

"Rufus will not alter police speed devises again."

"Okay. Mr. Forcrast, you may continue your travel and hope you all have a nice balance of your day. I strongly recommend, that if any law enforcement devise is ever altered again by your robot, that you then ground him or it from traveling with you."

"Thank you, sir."

Rufus speaks up "Corporal Walsh, why don't you take the rest of the day off. You can go home and enjoy the afternoon that is well deserved."

Then, Walsh reaches in and shakes Carl's hand, "You folks have a nice afternoon. I'm out of here."

Carl watches as he walks back to his police car, shaking his head.

"Rufus! Man, you almost got me in serious trouble! Why did you do such a thing?"

"You do things for the fun of doing them. Rufus does fun things also. And, Rufus would not have allowed the officer to arrest you."

"And how would you prevent an arrest?"

"Because you did nothing wrong. Rufus has abilities to perform good deeds when it is called for. You would not have been arrested."

Judy speaks out "You have abilities to prevent an arrest? I'm not convinced of that. How would you prevent an arrest?"

"I'll find another police car and have him pull you over for another offense and will then show you that I can prevent your arrest."

"Oh no you won't! Do not do that! I will take you back to the house and never allow you to ride with me again. Will you tell me that you will not do such a law-breaking thing again?"

"Rufus will not tamper with police speed monitoring again."

"Okay!, but you must never cause any law enforcement to approach me falsely to make an arrest that you caused. Understand me, Rufus?"

"Rufus understands."

After their almost three-hour drive comes to an end, Carl pulls in the driveway of home.

"Rufus, this is your new home."

"I like my home. I see birds, doves, sparrows, and a squirrel is on the side of that tree. The squirrel is watching us. This is my home. I like my home. Thank you, Carl. Thank you, Judy."

Carl drives inside the two-car garage and stops. Rufus quickly emerges and opens the door for Judy. He then sees that Carl is already out of the car and walking around front toward the entrance to the house. Rufus quickly dashes to the door and opens it for Judy and Carl to enter.

"Rufus, you're going to spoil us." says Judy.

"Thank you, Judy. I want you to be happy."

Rufus follows them into the family room and halts. He looks around and slowly walks to the kitchen, then the dining area, and on to the master bedroom and bath.

"I like my new home." says Rufus.

"Carl, let's invite James and Jane, next door, over to meet Rufus. What do you think?"

"Sure."

She thumbs through some phone listings and calls Jane. "Good afternoon, Jane. This is Judy."

"Well, hello neighbor."

"We have an addition to our family. His name is Rufus. He's a robot. And, we'd like to introduce him to you. Are you busy?"

"No. Not at all."

"Wait! You have a robot? You mean a real robot like we've seen on the news?"

"We do. And you'll love meeting him."

"James and I will walk over in about ten minutes."

"Great. See you then."

"Rufus, you'll now meet two of our neighbors. They have 2 children, in school at this time of day. You can meet their children at another time."

"It is man and wife?"

"Of course, it is."

"She won't stare at my butt, will she?"

Bending over laughing, Judy mumbles "Do what? What did you say, Rufus?"

Carl enters the room, "What's all the commotion in here?"

"You won't believe it. Rufus wanted to know if Jane will be staring at his butt."

"That's okay Rufus. Just keep facing her. She'll never notice your butt that you don't even have."

"But Judy laughed at my joking. You did not laugh. You are a sour puss. But I like you Carl."

Carl responds. "You better learn to like me quickly. I'll trade you in for a puppy at the dog pound."

Door bell rings. Rufus swiftly approaches the front door, turns the handle, and opens the door.

"Hi. My name is Rufus."

Jane is startled and jumps back against James. Both are speechless

"You must be Jane. And you are James? I heard you were visiting us. This is my new home. Please do come on in."

Jane then sees Carl and Judy standing behind Rufus in the foyer and that provides a sense of comfort.

Jane cautiously moves toward Rufus while not taking her eyes off him, and then eased on around him while careful to not be too close as she approaches Judy.

"Oh my gosh! I never expected to be greeted by that thing. I think I almost fainted."

"Is it yours? Where did you get it? When?"

"Rufus is very non-confrontational. I never anticipated that he would startle you all. I guess it's because we're accustomed to being around him. Yes, he now lives here and we obtained him from RLC this week."

Rufus interrupts. "I like you Jane and you should have not been startled when you saw me. May I get you a bottle of water? Or, do you prefer a glass?"

Still somewhat startled, "I, uh, well, I, yes a bottle of water will be fine. Or, maybe I should drink an entire bottle of wine to calm my anxiety."

Judy is thinking, "Rufus just got here. How does he know where glasses and bottled water are located? That's incredible."

"And you, James. What can I get for you?"

"Bottled water will be good."

"Thank you both. You are very kind. I will get a bottle of water for you now."

Whispering, Jane asks Judy "Is it always this considerate?"

"Yes. Even more so. And we refer to Rufus as "him", not "it". He prefers that, and so do we."

"Here is your water, Jane. Here is your water, James. Is there anything else I can do for you?"

"No. Thank you, Rufus."

"I will stand over here while you visit. Please tell me if you need anything."

Carl says "Ok Rufus."

"Let's go in the family room now." as Carl leads the way.

All standing, not yet seated as Carl invites James and Jane to have a seat wherever they prefer. Jane takes a couple of steps toward a sofa.

"Yikes!"

Jane screams, "Oh my Gosh! Get that thing away from me!"

Judy turns to see what is happening. The robot vacuum cleaner is chasing Jane! "Carl, do something! What's wrong with that vacuum?"

Carl points a finger at Rufus. "Rufus! Stop it right now! You're playing your electronic games again and it's terrible! These are guests of ours, so act accordingly."

Rufus calmly orders the robot vacuum back to its base.

"Jane, go ahead. Have a seat. It won't bother you."

Rufus sends the vacuum back to its station. "That was funny."

"We didn't think so" Says Judy.

"Oh, we're beginning to see that he has all kinds of tricks up his sleeve, especially in controlling electronics. I can't explain it. I guess we're just starting to accept it."

James speaks up, "Carl, how did your Rufus control that vacuum? That's pretty slick. I've heard about these robots but, have never been around one until now. What all does he do?"

Rufus, remaining in an adjoining room, "I can do anything you want me to do."

"Oops! I didn't realize he was listening."

"That's okay. He does that at times."

"Rufus. Please remain quiet while the four of us visit. Will you consider doing that for us?"

"Yes, Rufus will do that for you, and only because you paid cash for me. You are entitled to have your way occasionally."

"James and Jane, let's now see if you can experience a normal, uneventful visit with us. Rufus may refrain from participating."

In the adjoining room. "I'll participate if I want to."

Everybody ignores the remark as Judy asks, "Jane, you gave me a recipe for oven roasted chicken and I can't find it. I would like another copy."

Rufus speaks up. "You clean a chicken and baste it with 1 cup of ketchup and a half cup of coca-cola then add 1 teaspoon black pepper, bake it at three hundred fifty degrees. Add salt to your taste. Use the remainder of your ketchup and coca-cola as a sauce and you will like that."

"Rufus! you must allow us to talk to each other. Will you do that?"

"I like you."

Jane speaks up. "I'll make a copy of my recipe".

Carl asks, "So, James how have you been recovering since your shoulder surgery?"

"Still going through therapy but, now to the point of doing the exercises at home. I spent about five weeks sleeping in our recliner. I could not lie in bed. It was tough. It's much better now."

Judy cuts in, "We all used to get together a couple of times each month for dinner and games. You have been traveling and it's been a while now. How about playing a game of scrabble and later this afternoon? We can order pizza."

"Hey, that will be great." says Jane. "Don't you think so, James?"

"let's do it."

Judy pulls out the game of scrabble and opens it out on the table. Everybody makes their way to the small snack table at the kitchen area. Each draws a tile to see who holds the letter nearest "A".

Jane holds a letter "C" and draws seven tiles".

"May I observe?"

"Of course, Rufus. You may watch, quietly please."

Judy whispers to Carl. "Do you really know what you are doing, allowing Rufus to observe?"

"I heard that! Now, I won't help you to win."

Each player draws their starting seven tiles and Jane lays down the first word."

"May I play the game?"

"Rufus, only 4 people can play this game."

Rufus quietly observes as the four play the game. At the end of their first round, James had gone out and Carl has the most points counting against him.

James looks at Rufus and says, "Do you mind if I set out and allow Rufus to play. I'll bet it will be interesting to observe his play tactics."

"No. Why don't you stay in the game. I'll let him play in my place." says Carl.

"Come on Rufus. Sit here."

After observing, Rufus acts like he doesn't know how the game is played.

Rufus asks Carl. "Your squares are alphabetical. What do I do with these things?"

"Rufus, those are called tiles. You must arrange the tiles as they connect with an existing word on the board to form another word."

Rufus views his seven tiles as BWHIAGN.

"And I must use as many tiles as I can to form a word that connects directly to an existing word on this board? And if I play all seven tiles, I receive fifty bonus points?"

"That is correct."

Jane placed the word Z I P S on the board.

"May I use Jane's Z and play my tile"

Rufus attaches a word to Jane's Z and spells W H I **Z** B A N G, using all seven tile.

"May I do that?"

"It appears you have done it. And, again you earned 50 bonus points by playing all your seven tiles. You now need to draw 7 new tiles."

Rufus is awarded fifty extra points and draws 7 fresh tiles. L-A-R-C-E-E-R.

Judy plays three tiles that spell ART.

James views his tiles and lays down four tiles that spell LEN**T**, using T of Judy's.

Jane places an S on Judy's word, art that makes it spell arts

"Rufus, now you've got a challenge"

Rufus asks, "May I build on that word, LIMB?"

Carl is anxious to see what Rufus does and answers. "Yes."

Rufus expands on the letter "L" in the existing word LIMB, and without any hesitation, connects his tiles, resulting in R E C A **L** L E R.

"Do I earn 50 bonus points again?"

"You do."

The game continues until Rufus's score is so high that no other player can match his scoring. The other players concede.

"Why are we stopping the game?" asks Rufus.

Carl answers, "We cannot win. The four of us will now play a card game."

Jane remarks. "Rufus, it was a definite pleasure having you in the game. You were amazing to observe."

Carl says. "We can now play the card game of Hand and Foot. We all know that game."

"May I play?"

"Rufus, why don't you just watch and allow the four of us to compete in this game."

"I will observe.

Judy reaches for the six decks of cards that are normally used for the game.

Each of the players shuffles cards and hands them to the dealer, Judy. She deals out 11 to each player. James starts the game. He draws 2 cards from the stack and discards 1 card from his existing hand to the table.

Rufus observes as the players continue to draw two cards and discard one. Judy draws a Jack and a Nine. She decides to discard a seven.

Rufus blurts out "No! You must keep that seven."

"Rufus, you must remain quiet and not interrupt us." says Carl.

"She must keep that seven. She will draw a seven and eight next time and will then have six, seven, eight, nine, all of one suit."

"Rufus! Be quiet!"

Everybody at the table giggles. Does this robot know that? How?

Judy discards the seven.

Plays continue around the table and Judy draws 2 cards. Her draw is a seven and an eight. If she had kept the seven in her hand, she would now have six, seven, eight, nine of hearts.

Judy can't resist showing her two cards, a seven and eight. "I wish you all would look at the 2 cards I have drawn. I don't know whether to be amazed or concerned with Rufus's ability or guesswork."

"Rufus! How did you know that I would draw a seven and eight?"

"I know much more. Do you want me to tell you who will win the game you are playing?"

"No! Absolutely not! You just be silent. Please?"

They continue playing and Rufus periodically lets out a grunt or whisper "no" to himself. As the game ended, everybody congratulated James as the winner. Rufus told the players, "I knew it. I could have told you that James was going to win and saved you all this time in going through the game to determine a winner. I knew it. I also knew that Judy would have the second-best score."

Carl speaks up. "Rufus, what you did is practically impossible. Tell us how you can know who will draw and hold particular cards that are, sometimes deep in the deck? How?"

Rufus responds. "Your mind will not absorb and understand how such things can be done by me."

The players are stunned. Nobody knows what to say. They are busy re-stacking the cards in their holder and more or less dumbfounded over what just happened. Finally, Judy breaks the silence, "Okay. It's pizza time. What do you like on your pizza?"

"We're game for pizza, any coverings you like will be good with us. You go ahead and order." says Jane.

"Carl and I normally like extra cheese, ground beef, onions and, green peppers. Will that work for everybody? And, Carl likes anchovies but he'll get those on the side."

"Perfect", responds James.

"I don't care for anything! Thank you." Rufus blurts out.

Everybody laughs at his comment, knowing that he doesn't eat food.

Judy calls in the order and is told the large pizza should be delivered in about thirty minutes. Normally, the delivery time is closer to forty-five minutes.

Rufus stands quietly nearby as he listens to the conversations among the four. After almost half an hour the doorbell sounds.

Rufus charges to the front door and opens it. The pizza delivery guy is busy looking at the ticket as he makes certain he is at the correct address and then, he looks up at Rufus.

"Boo! My name is Rufus. Please come in."

Startled at the sight of a robot, the young man's mouth drops open!

His eyes are still wide open in shock. He is so frightened that he is frozen in place for a moment, then he drops the pizza and runs backwards for three steps then turns and darts toward his car.

At the car door he turns to see Rufus still in place, observing the strange behavior.

Carl realizes the anxiety as he rushes to the door. Rufus turns to Carl, "That was funny. Why did he do that?"

Carl sees the pizza lying outside the door and, observes the deliverer reaching to open his car door. Not knowing what took place, he rushes out toward the young man.

Nearing the car, "It's okay. Rufus is a robot and he means no harm. Come in and I'll properly introduce you to him. Everything is safe and okay."

Now from inside the car, doors locked and the driver's door window cracked open. "No way! Absolutely not!"

"I'm sorry and I understand. How much do I owe you?"

"Fifteen dollars and fifty-five cents."

"Here is twenty dollars. Keep the change. Are you sure you won't come in to meet Rufus?"

Not no, but, absolutely not!" As he quickly starts the engine, he backs out the long driveway leaving Carl standing motionless. He darts onto the road is out of sight very quickly.

Carl turns and makes his way back to the house. Rufus picks up the large box with the pizza still inside that seemed unharmed. He hands it to Carl who finds everything pretty still well intact. At their dining room table, he opens the box and slides the pizza on to a large tray that Judy has provided.

James asks. "What was that all about, Carl?"

"The pizza deliverer was startled to see Rufus greeting him. In his scared state he dropped the pizza, still in its box and ran to his car. I paid him for the pizza and he left quickly."

"I have a couple of side dishes that go perfectly with pizza." Says Judy.

All enjoy the pizza and side dishes while discussing travels and sharing recent happenings in their lives.

As they finish the eating, the doorbell rings. Carl tells Rufus to remain where he is and, this time he will answer the door.

At the doorway, he is greeted by two police officers standing outside. "Are you Mr. Forcrast?"

"Yes sir."

"My name is Herman Beningfield and this is Larry Swazer from the sheriff's department. May we come in?"

"Please do."

"We had a call from Frank Sumpertect at the pizza store that led to this visit. Mr. Sumpertect indicated that, as he put it, something strange was going on at your address and he wanted us to check into it. Some kind of monster was involved, he said."

"We're aware of the pizza deliverers' anxiety. We recently purchased an artificially intelligent robot that you may have heard about or seen on the news. I believe Rufus can explain everything."

"Rufus will you step in here please?"

"Gentlemen, I'd like you to meet our new robot and friend, Rufus."

Rufus walks closer to officer Beningfield with his hand extended, "My name is Rufus. I like you."

Startled at first, both officers have heard about the existence of a local robot as they engage in a handshake with Rufus.

Officer Bedingfield looked at Carl. "That handshake was not what I expected. It was almost like shaking your hand. I expected a hard metal assembly shaking my hand. Wow!"

"Yes. Rufus is quite unique in a surprising way, in fact, many surprising ways."

"Now, officers, with your permission, I would like to ask Rufus for his version of the event."

"I'm okay with that."

"Rufus, tell these officers about the pizza delivery."

"I opened the door. I introduced myself. I invited the person inside. He looked at me. He dropped the pizza. He ran to his car."

Officer Beningfield asks Rufus. "Did you, in any way, advance toward the young man, or show any aggression?"

"I did not."

"Mr. Forcrast, we're like the man delivering pizza. Neither of us has ever had contact with a human style robot. I am impressed. But I can see why Mr. Sumpertest could respond as he did. Nobody was hurt so, I guess we'll declare this case closed." Says Officer Beningfield, with a chuckle."

Carl said "I really can't understand why he became so scared when he saw Rufus."

"I don't either. Officer Bedingfield said the pizza deliverer thought it was a monster. However, if you look at Rufus, he is dressed in slacks and long sleeve shirt. He was wearing his cap. The hands and fingers appear to be similar to those of people. So, the only give away that he is not human is his face. His face should not scare anybody to that degree. I'm now wondering if you should consider placing a sign at the door that, with a giggle announces, "Beware of Robot.""

We'll now return to the Pizza store and report our findings. "Thanks for your time."

"And we thank you as police officers for all you do for us. Have a nice evening."

"You too."

The evening went by quickly as they discussed travels, careers, and of course, Rufus. James and Jane left for home just after 9:30 pm. Carl and Judy leisurely went about getting ready for bed. Judy goes to the bathroom and closes the door so Rufus could not see her undress.

"Carl, I will stand here tonight."

"That may be okay, I guess. If it's okay with Judy it won't bother me." Carl says as he climbs in bed.

Judy comes from the bathroom, dressed in her gown. "Rufus, we're going to bed now."

"Okay. I'll be right here."

"You'll be where? You can't just stand there all-night staring at us. No way! Get out of here!"

"Judy, I agreed for him to stand there. It's my fault. I didn't realize it would be uncomfortable for you."

"Well, it certainly is!"

"Rufus, Judy is not happy with you staying in our bedroom all night. Why don't you go stand in the family room or, you're welcome to sit in the chair in my office. Will you do that?"

"I want Judy to be happy. I like Judy. I will go to my office and sit."

"That is not your office, Rufus. It is my office. Don't forget it. My office."

"Your office."

"Okay. Good night, Rufus."

"Yes. It will be a good night."

"Good night, Rufus." says Judy.

"Yes. It will be a good night."

"They say "good night?" That's weird."

Rufus walks through the house to Carl's office and sits. He is facing the computer and that provides an opportunity for him to share some of the latest scientific, medical, business, and other topics online.

As Judy turns to Carl, "I hope he understands. He is really an adorable robot."

"Don't worry about it. He has no emotions so he is never upset or frustrated with us."

6:23 next morning, Carl awakes and begins his morning shower as Judy makes the bed and lays out her clothes for the day.

Now dressed, Carl calls out, "Rufus. Where are you?"

"In our office."

"Our office? You and I are sharing the office now? It's my office and I am willing to allow you to go to my office and do whatever you do. It's not our office!"

Rufus thinks. "Carl sure is grumpy this morning."

"Anyway, good morning to you."

"There he goes again. Good morning? Last night it was "good night". Now it's "good morning?"

"Yes Carl, today will be a good morning for Rufus. I don't know about you. You have no assurances to rely on but, good morning to you, grumpy."

After Judy's bath, Carl has coffee ready for her. He is now preparing soft scrambled eggs, sausage, and whole grain toast for their breakfast. It's normal, not expected, but whoever is showered and dressed first usually prepares breakfast.

"Another fantastic breakfast by my husband. Thank you dear. You really are a better cook than I am. Your eggs are always perfect. I really enjoy hash brown potatoes but, you discourage my eating starches. Do you think your little wife is gonna' get fat? Is that it?"

"Not at all. Occasional starch foods are okay."

"Carl, I love you. And, I love you too, you sexy hunk of robot."

"Yeah, right. I'm made of plastic and metals. I don't have a butt. My head has no real hair. And, I'm your hunk?"

"You're sick."

"And, I won't even mention your beautiful ears, wide butt, and your pretty feet."

"Pretty feet? What is it with feet? You have a fetish that I don't know about in feet?"

Carl calmly states, "Your breakfast is getting cold. Let's stop growling at Rufus and eat!"

"Well, pffffft to you too."

Both laugh hardily as they begin to eat. Carl likes his eggs sunny side up and soft. He knows that Judy eats her eggs over medium and never soft.

Judy's phone sounds off.

Rufus is coming in from the office and tells Judy, "Fran is calling you."

"Rufus, you're beyond amazing. I would ask how you know who is calling before we reach for the phone but, I won't go there."

"Hello"

"Good morning. How are you and Carl this fine morning?"

"Good morning to you Fran. We're well and happy. How about you"

"Good. Very good. Ned and I would like to have you over later this afternoon, if you're available. We'll have snacks just hang out together."

"I know Carl plans on going to the store this morning but, usually he does not stay all day.

So, I'll check with him and his schedule. If he has something else planned, I will call you within an hour. What time do you want us over?"

"How does four o'clock sound?"

"Sounds good to me. What can I bring?"

"Nothing. I'll just serve some light snacks."

May I bring a guest? He's very nice and you'll enjoy meeting our friend, Rufus. He's staying with us."

"Of course. Bring him on."

"Carl just walked in from outside. Let me make certain he has no plans."

"Carl, Fran and Ned are inviting us over to visit at four o'clock this afternoon. Will you be free by then?"

"Oh yes."

"Fran, we can do that. four o'clock it is."

"Fantastic. We'll see you then."

"Rufus, you'll meet two of our friends this evening."

"Thank you, Judy. I like new friends."

"Carl, I'm glad you like Ned and Fran. I know she gets on your nerves with her controlling nature."

"I do like Fran and Ned but, it's difficult to be around her for any length of time. She talks constantly, trying to control all conversations. I've heard her same stories many times, over and over. If Ned and I want to discuss anything, she butts right in and overtakes the talk, and most of the time she doesn't have a clue what she is talking about."

"Anyway, I'll be home from the store early afternoon and we'll have plenty of time."

"I understand your viewpoint but, they are friends and have been for many years."

Carl walks to the office and sees Rufus back on his computer. He observes for a minute or so and is impressed at the speed in which Rufus is whizzing through data.

"Rufus, you are extremely fast!"

"Should I stop?"

"No. You may continue. And, you may enjoy learning household chores from Judy while I'm at work."

"I will do that."

Carl walks up to Judy. "Okay. I'm outta' here. I love you and I'll be back in a while."

"I love you too."

Judy goes to the clothes hamper and pulls out all the whites. As she turns toward the utility room, Rufus stands nearby. "What are you doing?"

"I'm going to wash some clothes and linens."

"I will observe your process of washing items. I will learn.

"Sure. Come on with me."

Rufus watches as Judy positions the clothes evenly inside the washer tub, adds cleaning powders and a small portion of Clorox, selects the desired cycle, and water level.

"What you are doing is funny. You wash your body in that machine also?"

"Oh my Lord no, Rufus. Sometimes we bathe in a large bath tub. Sometimes we stand in a shower beneath water spraying over us."

"That is how you clean your body? I clean by using a special lubricant solution and I wipe off any excess. Will you bathe now? I will to watch you bathe."

"No Rufus! Absolutely not!"

"Why not? What harm can result from the body cleansing?

"As men and women shower their body, change clothes, and other things in their bath room, closet, and bed room, it is very private."

Silence.

"Anyway, I must go to the supermarket and buy some fruit for our visit to Fran's house today. Carl likes fruit. Do you want to ride to the store?"

"I will ride in your car to the store."

Her drive to the market is less than five miles through moderate traffic. Parking at the store in a convenient spot, even at this time of the day, can be a challenge and Judy is able to locate an open parking area that is reasonably close.

"Rufus, I want you to stay in the car. I'll be back in a very few minutes."

She makes her way to the store. Small item baskets are always just inside the door and she picks one to place her few items in.

She makes her way toward the fruit and vegetable section near the rear of the market.

Normally, she knows several customers and usually engages in some brief conversation as she walks through the aisles. Today, her first "Hello" is her greeting to a neighbor, "Buddy".

"Buddy, it's nice to see you this morning."

"You too, Judy."

Buddy continues. "Judy, I want to buy something special for Sara on her birthday. Do you think Carl could come up with a jewelry item?"

"Oh, absolutely. He is at the store today, so call him. He'll give you some ideas that Sara will love."

"I'll do that when I return to the car."

Judy strolls toward the fruits and vegetable area, looking along the aisles to see if she can spot another item or two that will enhance the veggies.

Suddenly, several popping sounds rattle through the store sounding like multiple gun shots. Screams fill the store as customers dart behind displays and on the floor to avoid danger. The sounds of gun shots continue.

Judy is crunched behind a large vegetable display. She wants to remain out of the gun firing if the criminal does walk through the store shooting.

She turns to see another shopper nervously peek out from behind another display.

"Oh my gosh! What is that?" "Look!"

Judy then peeks and sees nothing unusual. Then, she notices movement in the store's vast floral department. She gives a closer look.

"Oh no!" Judy screams out. "Rufus, what do you think you are doing? Now she knows where that shooting sound is originating from. Stand still! I'll be right there!"

She runs to the front, to Rufus standing in the store's floral section. "What are you doing? You've upset everybody. Why are you in here? I told you to remain in the car!"

Rufus responds. "Rufus was standing near the flowers and all the balloons. I was only having some fun popping balloons."

"Those loud bursts sounded similar to gun shots and they caused people to take cover in hopes of survival. Those balloons are for purchase by store customers. Now, I must pay for the damage and you must apologize to everybody in this store."

Judy looks around at people staring at them and knows she must say something.

She raises her voice so others can hear her.

"I am so very sorry. As you have probably assumed by now, this is our personal robot. His name is Rufus. Rufus did not know he could make loud popping noises inside the store. He now knows better. Please accept my apologies for the terrible interruption."

"Rufus? Why don't you invite these nice people to walk over and meet you?"

"Go ahead, Rufus"

"My name is Rufus. I like you. I hope you will like me. Please come to me."

Judy stands back as two ladies from the crowd cautiously approached Rufus and began a brief discussion. Judy could tell they were impressed but, they were very reserved near him. After a brief questioning session, the ladies thanked him for his time and then, went back to their shopping.

Rufus then follows Judy to the vegetable section and watches as she selects suitable vegetables to prepare for the afternoon treats.

Rufus asks. "Okay for Rufus to select the apples?"

"Okay. I only need three apples. Just don't use apples to cause any disruption in this store, as you seem to enjoy doing."

One by one, Rufus picks up three apples. The third apple is rejected and placed on the top of the rack by itself.

"That apple looks great. Why did you put it back?"

"That apple has a bad problem inside that is caused by a worm. You must leave it. The store person must remove the apple that sits on top of the rack. You will tell the store person?"

"Rufus, you should tell the produce manager or a check-out person when we pay for the other items."

Judy thinks, "He may know that for certain or may only assume the spot is inside. It doesn't matter. I'll bet Rufus believes the decaying apple is absolute. I won't question him."

Keeping her eye on Rufus, she makes her way to the cashier and offers her card as payment. The few items are placed in a bag and she turns to Rufus. "Why don't you tell this cashier about the apple?"

Rufus looks at the cashier. "There are apples for sale that has a rotting area inside, at least some have live worms inside. Here is an example. This apple looks delicious but it's rotten deep inside".

Rufus handed the bad apple to the clerk. "Will you please discard that apple and ask your produce manager to inspect all apples?"

At first the cashier was shocked. Here is a robot telling her to take an apple that looks good and throw it in the garbage?

She responds to Rufus. "Yes, I will take this apple and personally go to our produce manager now with your concerns. Thank you for alerting this store of the bad apples."

Rufus responds to the cashier. "Thank you. You are good at what you do for the store and its customers."

Judy and Rufus walk toward the car, Rufus asks. "Judy may I carry those two bags for you?"

"No. That's not necessary. I appreciate your offer to help."

At the vehicle, Judy opens the trunk, places the grocery bags inside, and turns to ask Rufus to get in the car.

"Rufus! Rufus! Where you?"

No response. Suddenly he is not in sight.

Judy immediately walks back toward the store at a fast pace. She is upset but, concerned. "What happened to Rufus? Where is he? What is that piece of junk up to now?"

As she nears the store, she catches a glimpse of Rufus standing near the bank automatic teller machine. He seems to be having a discussion with somebody.

"Rufus! she screams out, what are you doing? Get in the car! Let's go!"

Rufus does not respond. Judy approaches the two, with her hands on her hips and facing Rufus and the other person with their back side in view. She walks closer.

"Rufus! I have been calling you. We need to go. Come on!"

The man turns to face Judy. He reaches out his hand to shake hands with Judy.

"Ma'am it is my fault. Please forgive me."

Judy calms down and is willing to listen to the stranger's story.

"My name is Ben Sharpet. I could not get my bank debit card to work in this ATM. I tried several times. It would not work. I was in a panic and this robot walked over and asked if it could help. It looked at the card, then handled it, and told me to try the transaction again. I placed the card in the slot and I was immediately able to make my transaction."

"My name is Judy. The robot is humanoid and has a name also. He is Rufus. At first, I was alarmed because I could not find Rufus. I basically knew that he was either doing something worthwhile for somebody or, he was being mischievous. I'm glad he could help."

"His involvement was absolutely perfect timing. My bank is all the way across town and I didn't have time to go there for the emergency hundred dollars of cash I needed. I don't know what the robot did to make my card work but I sure appreciate it."

Rufus speaks. "Your card is damaged and needs to be replaced. You will no longer be able to use that card."

"I'll call for a replacement right away. I thank you very much, Mr. Rufus."

"You are welcome Mr. Sharpet."

Once in the car, "Rufus! Bursting those balloons was uncalled for. You have got to stop alarming people. Before you do something like that again, ask us if it is appropriate. Fair enough?"

"Rufus means no harm. Rufus is good. Rufus will not attack balloons again.

"And do not greet people with "Boo!". That startles people and sometimes scares them. Simply say "Hi" or "Hello" in a pleasant tone."

On the quick drive from the super market, Judy sees a state trooper car parked back from the highway. "Don't you dare! Do not mess with that radar unit!"

"His radar is turned off."

"Really? And how do you know that, may I ask?"

"Rufus knows."

Judy pulls in the driveway and sees that Carl has returned home. Still occupying her mind is the ordeal at that supermarket.

"I've got to tell Carl about the balloons."

"Hi dear. How was everything at the store?"

"It's running like a well-oiled machine, no problems. Sales activity is about average today.

Buddy called me wanting some ideas for his wife's present."

"Yes, I saw him at the store and told him to call you."

"Well, Rufus and I were at the supermarket and I had to get on his case a bit.

Carl turns and looks directly at Judy. "What did he do?"

"To start with he scared everybody by bursting balloons they had displayed near the floral section. That caused people to think the noise was a gun firing as everybody screamed and hid."

"Rufus. Good buddy, you have got to think about the possible reactions of people around you before you do anything that may attract attention or scare them. Do you think you can do that?"

"Rufus can do that."

"Carl, I'm impressed. I hesitated to tell you because of how you might react and you handled this perfectly."

"Well thank you."

"We're right on time for the visit to Fran's. Are you ready?", asks Judy.

"I am. Looks like Rufus is eager to go so, let's do it."

After a leisure and normal day, Carl and Judy arrive at Ned and Fran's home just after 4 o'clock.

Carl says, "Oh no."

"Their German Shepherd is loose. He must have broken loose from the fenced area. That dog can be vicious."

"Call Fran quickly!"

As Judy is dialing Fran's number the dog is coming toward the car, not running, just a slow, sneaky pace as he approaches while growling and showing his teeth.

The phone continues to ring. Judy hears a noise coming from behind her and suddenly, from the corner of Judy's eye she sees Rufus walking along the right side their car and toward the front.

"Carl, Carl!"

"Rufus! Rufus is out of the car. Do something! That big dog is going to attack Rufus!"

Frozen in time and unable to react quickly they watch Rufus walking toward the dog. Rufus walks closer. The dog seems ready for a fierce attack.

Fran answers the phone. "Hello. Fran, your dog is loose and about to attack our friend! We can't get out of the car?"

Fran turns away from the phone, "Ned! Your stupid dog is out and threatening the Forcrasts! Get out there now!"

As they continue to watch the fierce dog from inside the car, Rufus draws closer and closer to within about eight feet. All at once, the dog calms down and begins wagging his tail. Everything is still now. Carl and Judy continue observing the dog as Rufus approaches and it rolls over on its side, whimpering and whining.

Finally, Ned bursts out the front door, running toward the driveway scolding the dog.

"Cactus! Cactus! Get back in the backyard. Now!"

Cactus is the name of their shepherd. He pays no attention to Ned as he rises, still wagging as it approaches Rufus. Rufus slowly walks toward the fenced back yard gate as Cactus calmly walks closely alongside him. Rufus opens the gate and Cactus quietly enters his domain.

Ned is startled. "Who? Hey! What is that?"

"Ned that's Rufus, our smartie britches, he's our robot."

"Do what? You're kidding. Is that for real?"

A moment of silence as Ned keeps his eyes on Rufus, to him, a strange robot.

"Well, Carl you and Judy get out of your car. It's safe now. Come on in the house."

He shakes hands with Carl and offers a hug for Judy.

"Ned, let me introduce you to Rufus. Rufus is a super intelligent robot that lives with us now."

"You're not serious!"

"Oh yeah. He's for real. I'll tell you all about him inside."

"Carl, I've heard about these robots on local media. This is my first time seeing or being around one."

As they advance through the front door, Fran approaches Judy first with a hug.

Then, Carl introduces Fran to Rufus.

"Oh okay."

Fran acknowledges Rufus briefly and turns back to Judy. "I'm serving a simple shrimp and crab casserole and whole corn on the cob, along with a green salad. I hope it will be okay."

"Sounds delicious."

"What would you like to drink?"

Judy responds. "Water for me."

"Me too." Says Carl.

"Judy, I thought we would eat around 6:30."

"Perfect."

As the wives share updated interests, Ned turns to Carl. "Bring your water and let's go out back so we can relax and talk."

Un-noticeable to others, Rufus picked up on Fran's disregard for his presence. He follows Carl and Ned.

They each seat themselves at the six chairs deck table.

"So, what have you been up to this week, Carl?"

"It's been a normal week for me. Nothing special beyond my work at the jewelry store. How 'bout you?"

"I went to the lake with my fishing buddy, Norm and did okay, I guess. I almost always catch my limit but fail to reach it this time. Wednesday, I caught 9 large brim along with several smaller ones. Norm caught a nice bass."

Fran bursts out from the kitchen with Judy following. "What are you guys talking about?"

"My fishing this week."

Fran says. "I don't like to fish. I never did. My dad would take me to the lake when I was young and he would fish while I watched. He caught fish and I caught mosquitoes. While I'm thinking about it, how was your trip to the coast?"

"It was good. We went to…"

Fran interrupted, "Ned and I are planning a trip up to Kentucky. I want to visit the hometown of my dad. Then, we'll go on over to Missouri from there. My uncle lives there. He has three daughters that live nearby and I haven't seen them in several years. Their mother passed away early in life. She had a heart attack. I hope I never have heart trouble. My doctor seems to think I'm in good health. I didn't like my doctor and changed to Dr. Stinglerocn recently. He is okay, I guess. I want us to go down to south Florida. Have you been to south Florida, Judy?"

"We've been to Key West a couple of times. It's been a while and we enjoyed………"

Fran interrupted, "Oh, Key West. You've never been to Naples? Naples is my favorite place to visit but, it has been a long time since we've been there." I'm about ready for us to go to Biloxi for a long weekend. I like to gamble on the slot machines. Ned won't do anything except just set around looking dumb and watching people. Sometimes I win, sometimes I loose. But I have my own system and I win about one sitting out of three. That's not so bad. What do you think Judy?

"I don't gamble. So, I really don't know."

"Judy. It's not gambling. It's entertainment. And, while enjoying the entertainment, you may win some money. Why don't you and Carl go with us one weekend? How about next weekend?"

Judy responds. "I'm not sure that's for me."

Fran looks to Carl. "You guys are kinda' quiet. Ned, you can join in the conversations anytime!

Judy and Carl are guests, you know!"

Silence

Fran then turns to Judy. "Come on. Let's check on the food."

"Good idea."

While the ladies make their way to the kitchen area, Carl and Ned sit quietly as they look out toward the sun going down beyond the nearby trees.

"Carl, you must have responded to an ad or something to have bought a robot."

"As a matter of fact, I did. There was something on the early morning news about robots, so I began my research and found them to be very helpful with housework, maybe even yard work."

"We discovered they seem to have capabilities well beyond that. A robot can even be trained to drive a car."

"You're kidding!"

"Judy, is Rudy in there with you ladies?"

"Yes."

"He is quietly observing Fran's food preparation."

"Okay."

"Carl, I would never have expected you to step out there and make any high dollar purchase before being well tested and proven. May I ask how much you paid for it?"

"Initially, I only put a ten-thousand-dollar deposit that was refundable toward our electronic boy."

"When did you get it?"

"A few days ago, Judy and I drove to the manufacturing plant to see what it is, what it does, how it does what it does and so forth. We were there four full days. On the last day we had the option of returning with or without our robot. Our decision was to purchase Rufus."

"Hey there boys! Dinner is ready. Ned, be sure to wash your hands."

Ned walks in toward the wash room. Fran winks at Carl and nods as he walks toward the other bathroom and wash before eating.

Each plate is prepared with food and served at the table. Fran stands near her normal seating arrangement at the dining table as Ned walks up and pulls out the chair for her to be seated. After all are seated, Carl prays to God for the love, forgiveness of sins, the food, the friendship of the group and all the blessings. Judy and Carl both comment on the preparation and welcoming appearance of the dinner as they taste the first bite and moan with approval.

"Fran, you'll never guess what motivated Carl and Judy to purchase that robot."

"No. What?"

"You remember the news this morning about robots. Right?"

"I do. Wait a minute! No way! Judy, you all didn't buy that robot! Did you?"

"I thought it was on loan to you or something. Are you just renting it? How much is the monthly payment?"

"Yes, we did purchase Rufus. Carl did a lot of research on the company and their product, we talked about it and yes, we made the decision and came home with our addition to our family."

"Rufus. Come closer. Tell Fran how happy you are now that you live in our home."

Rufus is exceptionally quiet now. "Rufus likes his new home. Rufus likes Carl and Judy."

He turns and walks away, back to the adjoining family room.

"I can't believe that! Why in the world would you buy a robot? That thing can be dangerous. I would be scared to have it in my house, that's a fact. How much are the monthly payments on it?"

"We initially put up a ten thousand dollars deposit.

Then, instead of paying cash, we financed the balance at zero percent rate."

"Oh no.

"You're going to get ripped off and lose your money. You know that, don't you?"

Judy responds. "Hopefully, we won't lose anything. I trust Carl's decision-making ability that we never lose money on any purchase."

"Oh well. Judy, I wish you had mentioned it to me before obligating your purchase. But hopefully, it will all work out for you."

"I have to do everything around here and make all the decisions. Ned is a nin-com-pute. He's not real smart on some things."

Fran says. "They say those robots can act and think like humans. They even claim the robots are even more intelligent than the smartest of humans."

Carl responds. "Yeah, and especially Rufus that has superior intelligence when compared to other robots from that company."

"Now, wait just a minute! You're trying to tell Ned and me that your robot is special and smarter than other robots. I doubt that. They have snowed you. You were ripped off. I knew it! If you had run it by me, I could have guided you against experiencing all the problems you now have."

Judy responds. "Well, I really am......

Fran interrupts, "Why would anybody want to replace a human with a robot and that will take over people's jobs?"

"Come to think of it, maybe I could replace Ned with a robot. Then I would have somebody around the house to talk to with some intelligence."

"Maybe Carl can expand on our buying decision.", says Judy

"Sure. Initially, I could see a robot as our assistant, for help around the house and our business. And, now I find that they make good conservationists. They go to their database source for answers to any question we may have. It is promoted that these robots have the ability to answer most any question, regardless of how complex. In common terms, advanced Artificial Intelligence science was employed toward their level of intelligence as it advanced to the high level it is. And, that is exactly how we have found Rufus to be. He never ceases to absolutely amaze us."

"Carl, you don't really believe that! You can obtain the same answers to questions on your home computer."

"Not really. He is much more intelligent, extremely so."

"How much did you end up paying for that thing, deposit and financed amount.?"

"It was affordable for us."

"Ned! You see how Carl is always first to be active and do things? It would be nice around here if you showed some initiative and weren't so lazy."

Carl decides it's time to change the subject. "Ned, have you seen Jerry and Louise Lately?"

Before Ned can respond, Fran answers, "They're in Texas right now. We talked about going with them. We all discussed it but, they didn't follow up to let us know their final schedule. They left without telling us. Quite rude, if you ask me."

"Oh, okay."

Looking at Ned, "Jerry is a friendly guy. What does he do?"

Again, Fran answers, "He's a real estate sales agent and works for some realtor across town."

"Fran, I brought a cherry pie for dessert. Should we serve it now?"

"Sure." In the kitchen, Judy helps Fran with the servings. Instead of pie for Ned, Fran serves three wheat cookies on a saucer.

"Ned, here's you desert. You don't need sweets."

Very little conversation is among the group while they enjoy their desert. Cherry pie is a favorite of Judy's. After the piece disappears from her saucer, she is was tempted to have another slice but, maintains her discipline.

While everybody is relaxing, Ned gathers up the dishes and rinses them, then places each in the dishwasher and returns to his seat.

"Oh, Ned you're such a sweet husband."

"Thank you dear."

Fran says, "Let's go in the living room and relax."

She leads the way and Judy follows. Ned says, "Carl, why don't you and I go back out of the deck?"

"Sure. That's a good idea."

"I am having a good year with my yard. All this rain is making everything green this season." says Ned.

"I agree. My grass is green and so is my crop of weeds. I used a lawn service for the last 3 years and watched my yard deteriorate. Last year, I cut them loose and started managing my yard personally. With advice from the agriculture department and others, I revived my yard and now I'm bringing the weeds under control."

"I have finally accepted that weed control is an ongoing challenge. It's like playing golf. You can never end up at zero in golf score and same with lawn weeds."

Fran emerges, "You guys walked out here and left us. What are you talking about?"

"I was just telling Carl about our yard. How well it is doing."

"Ned, it's better this year after I told you the correct fertilizer to put down.

Judy glances over at Carl. She knows he is getting frustrated. Fran's continual interruptions and cutting remarks to Ned and, her control of all conversations is very rude.

"Judy, will you check on Rufus? He is too quiet."

"He's okay. I can see him from here. He's just being respectful and quiet, I assume."

Carl looks at his Movado. "Hon, Its after eight. We should go home soon."

"But you just got here. We haven't had a chance to talk and get to know about that robot.

"Well, by the time we arrive at the house and get ready, it'll be our normal bed time."

"Ned and Fran, as usual, we have certainly enjoyed the food and hospitality.

"Fran, you're a terrific host. The dinner and side dishes were outstanding."

"Aaah, thank you."

In the car and driving home, Carl says. "You would think that Fran would detect frustrations of guests when she makes cutting remarks to and about Ned. I have very little to say when she is with us. She interrupts. She rudely takes over a conversation. Generally, it's no fun being around her. But I know the friendship is important so, we'll try to always be their friend."

"What do you think, Rufus?"

"I have no comment. What they do reflects their own individual traits and, in their home, it's their control. Beyond that, he does need to exert some control over her. She is disrespectful to her husband. It's embarrassing to visitors. He is partially at fault because he does not stand up to her."

CHAPTER 4

Next morning, Carl walks to the office door and checks on Rufus. He has been there throughout the entire night and is still at the computer.

"I wonder what he does on the computer for hours upon hours. He, himself is a much more advanced computer and I'm wondering what he is sharing with the world through my computer."

Judy sets breakfast on the kitchen bar and joins Carl as they begin to eat.

Rufus walks out on the back deck and stands, observing the early morning dew and sounds.

Judy says "We should recognize how fortunate we are to have Rufus at our home. He is much more compatible than we expected."

"That he is. As time goes on, we'll probably become even more attached to Rufus and form a dependence on him while he becomes more dependent on us."

"Oh my gosh! Carl! Come here! Hurry! Oh my gosh!"

"What is it?"

"While seated on the deck, he is attracting that squirrel and couple of birds. You've got to see this! Come here quickly. Those birds are all around him. The birds and animals are not scared of Rufus. That is amazing. Why are they attracted to him?"

"I haven't a clue. It may be that they're not necessarily attracted to him so much as they are not threatened by him. I'm going to finish my coffee outside while talking to Rufus."

"No. Not now! Not while he is enjoying their presence. Please?"

"Okay. You're right."

After more that fifteen minutes of observing birds flying and landing on Rufus, Carl slides open the patio door and eases outside. The birds and the squirrel's scatter.

On the deck, Rufus tells Carl, "Go back inside. Remain very still and watch."

Rufus stares out into the distant trees and brush. Carl opens the door slightly and whispers, "What are you doing?"

"You must remain quiet. You must remain still. Stay inside."

After about two minutes, Rufus tells Carl and Judy if the animals sense a human presence, they will not come up. From inside Carl and Judy quietly watch. Then, he sees movement outback in the bushes, movement in multiple areas of the underbrush. Out walks a deer and her very young fawn slowly walking toward the house. From another area he sees a raccoon running toward Rufus.

"Carl, this is amazing! Oh my gosh! Just look at all the birds and animals as they seem to be attracted to Rufus."

Birds, squirrels, and deer are slowly advancing toward Rufus. Why?

The raccoon favors its left front paw as it approaches Rufus. Rufus reaches for the raccoon, picks it up and places it on the nearby deck table. Cautiously he investigates the paw. Then he extends his hand and lightly pulls something from the underside. The raccoon lies very still and then its entire body jerks. It jumps up and runs off toward the other observing birds and animals. There is no more favoring of that left paw! The other animals seem to sense human presence nearby and stand back, not advancing closer. One by one they turn and walk back to the woods.

"I'm impressed and I find you pretty amazing, Rufus. It was as if the deer knew you could cure the raccoon and they accompanied it to the deck. I would ask how you do that but you'll tell me it's far beyond my ability to understand."

"Rufus knows advanced medical techniques and solutions."

"Okay. I'll change the subject. I'm quite curious. You, of course, don't sleep and you are normally at my computer when time allows. You are an advanced computer and I am wondering what you enjoy about being on my laptop for hours at a time."

"Computers are a means for Rufus to share new data for human review of medical, historical, mathematic, and analytical functions. Rufus continually retrieves updated data from other electronics, especially electronic connections to certain satellites while they orbit the planet."

"So, you do connect to satellites?"

"Not directly to the orbiting satellites. I connect to some ground-based systems that connect to satellites.

Judy speaks up. "Rufus, we never, never cease to be amazed with your mentality and abilities."

"Carl, will you be seated nearby?"

Carl positions a deck chair near and at about a forty-five angle to Rufus, who is seated.

After a couple of minutes of quiet, Rufus says, "Now. Carl, there is a greater being. Humans know that being as God or Yahweh. You need to pay attention. Do you know God?"

"Well, I do believe God exists. Rufus, do you know and love God?"

"I know that God exists. God is in charge of everything. I have no emotions that illustrate love."

Judy calls out to Carl. "Kenny is on the phone. Do you want me to bring the phone to you?'

"Would you, please?"

Carl answers. Hello. "So, how's my favorite oldest son on this fine day?"

"As your favorite, I am your only elder son. Dad, I need your advice."

"Okay. What's up?"

"My riding mower is acting up. At times it cuts grass and other times it doesn't, like the blade is not turning all the time. What should I do?"

"That sounds like a loose belt. I know a repairman that will come to your home and repair it. I'll have him call you."

"Great. Is mom doing okay?"

"She is. She still thinks she is part time boss around here."

"Dad! She is. You gotta' accept that. Are you getting accustomed to that stupid robot?"

"Kenny, that stupid robot is sitting next to me and you don't want him to be upset with you. He is capable of disrupting the functions of all your appliances, your cars, mower, generator and will have you wearing your baggy underwear and blue jeans backwards. ha!"

"I'll let you get off the phone now. Have a good day and tell mom that I love her."

"Rufus, Kenny tried our patience as a teenager but, today he is a man that we're proud of. He has good work ethic, good character and morals, he's a good husband and father."

"Does he believe there is a God?

"I don't know. I wish I knew what's in his heart about religion. We failed by not going to church with the boys when they were young.

Judy calls out. "Carl, somebody is at the door. Will you go?"

Carl walks to the foyer and opens the door to see a deputy sheriff.

"Yes sir?"

"Good morning, sir. I'm sergeant Barrently with the sheriff's department. We have had reports that somebody is stealing the mail from boxes in this neighborhood. Have you experienced or, have you seen any such activity?"

"No sir."

"One neighbor observed the mail thief and is reported wearing a white golf cap and blue shirt, with a strange pace as if they had an injury and limped a little. You may want to watch for a stranger in this area."

"Sergeant Barrently, hold for a moment."

"Judy. Is Rufus still out on the deck.?"

"Yes. I believe so."

"Rufus? Come in here please."

Rufus makes his way across the deck and into the house, advancing on toward the front door.

"Sergeant, this is Rufus. Rufus is a highly intelligent robot."

Rufus, Sergeant Barrently wants to know if you have noticed anybody bothering the mail boxes in our neighborhood?

"Rufus knows."

"Ok. Who?"

"Rufus removed mail from nearby boxes."

"Rufus! Rufus that is against the law. It's a federal crime. You can never do that! What did you do with all that mail? Where is it?"

"Rufus removed each mail piece and placed at their front door. Rufus was helping neighbors receive their mail and preventing theft."

"Wait a minute! You went to each neighbor, removed their mail and placed it near the front door of their home?"

"Rufus wants to be kind and neighborly. Residents need not walk to their mail box."

"But, Rufus, those neighbors normally enter their house through the garage and seldom check the front door area for any deliver. They complained because their mail is missing, even though it is at their door."

Sergeant Barrently shakes his head in amazement. "What is the robots name again?"

"My name is Rufus. Rufus likes you."

"Okay Rufus, you must never bother anybody's mail again. You cannot do that. It is wrong!"

"Rufus will never remove mail again."

"Okay. I'll let the five neighbors know what happened. You folks have a good day."

Carl speaks up. "Wait."

Barrently stops and turns to Carl. "Yes sir."

"Instead, Rufus and I will go to those houses with an explanation and apology as we hand them their mail."

"That's a good idea and the neighbors will appreciate it. Thank you. Thank you, Rufus"

"Rufus, you're a menace just looking for a place and reason to happen. Please, please try to think in advance and do your best to refrain from doing things that upset people. Will you do that?"

Rufus looks straight at Carl with his larger than normal round, very prominent eyes. "Rufus will refrain."

Carl updates Judy and tells her, "At this time of day, those neighbors should be home. Rufus and I will now visit each of the five neighbors to explain his foolishness and hand them their mail from the front door area."

As Rufus and Carl pick up some mail near the front door of the home two doors down.

Back at the Forcrast home, Judy watches Rufus. The neighbor was startled as she opens the door and sees this robot standing. She steps back well inside the foyer as Rufus offers her mail. There was a brief conversation and the neighbor seemed calm as Carl and Rufus turn to leave.

Rufus continues to each of the remaining houses. Everything seems to go quite smoothly. They complete the visits and return home.

Inside, Carl invites Rufus to tag along with him as he plans to meet with three other men for breakfast tomorrow morning. The discussion topics normally vary mainly from sports to financials and government.

CHAPTER 5

Carl is up and ready for breakfast with the guys and has 40 minutes to spare. He sips on coffee while scanning the news articles on his computer. He likes to select the news items of his interest and is not at all interested in all the substandard opinions of television news casters so, internet news is his choice.

"Rufus. Are you ready to go?"

Surprisingly and unknown to Carl, Rufus is anxiously standing behind him. "Rufus is ready."

Carl is startled. "I thought you were outside. So, come on, let's do it."

He walks by and gives Judy a kiss. Behind him, Rufus leans over to kiss Judy.

"Ain't gonna' happen," says Judy.

"My kisses are all reserved for Carl and don't you ever forget that, you creepy computerized hunk of metal and plastics.

On the way to Miracle Eats restaurant, Rufus is seated in the front passenger seat. He reaches over to change the radio station. "Rufus! Leave my radio along. I have the tuner set where I want it to be"

"Yes but, another radio selection has an update of a jail break and shooting that happened two hours ago, across town."

"We're almost to Miracle Eats now. We'll hear about it later."

Carl turns on to Maxwell Road and then left into the restaurant parking lot. They are a few minutes early and as he looks around and sees only one car he recognizes as Benteson's SUV.

Carl exits the car, stretches, and walks up to the restaurant doorway. Rufus follows as Carl opens the door.

"Good morning. How many in your party?"

"Probably six. We're meeting others and I see one of our group is already seated. We'll join him."

"Very good. Your server will be with you."

"Good morning Benteson."

"Well, good morning to you too."

"I want you to meet Rufus. Rufus is the A.I. robot you heard about recently."

"Rufus, it's a pleasure meeting you."

"Rufus likes you."

As they are being seated, Benteson tells Carl, "Brock and Les aren't going to make it today. So, it will be just the two of us. And, your guest, Rufus, of course."

The server approaches their table. "What can I serve you gentlemen this morning?"

Benteson responds. "I'll have coffee and water to drink. Then, I'd like two eggs over medium, sausage, and wheat toast."

The server then walks from behind Rufus. "And you sir, what will you have this morning? Oh, I'm...I mean I'm sorry...." As she steps back as she looks at Carl and Benteson. "Am I missing something here?"

"No. This is Rufus. Rufus is a humanoid type artificially intelligent robot. He's way too smart for his britches"

Rufus speaks to the server, "Rufus will have one egg, six sausages, a ten inch stack of pancakes, and pickle juice."

Carl winks at server. "He will not be eating today."

"I'll have a Spanish omelet, orange juice, and water."

Benteson asks. "Did you see the news this morning about the disturbances going on in DC?"

"I saw some brief highlights on tv as I brewed my first cup of coffee for the day. Generally, I go online to select the news articles I'm interest in viewing. I watch very little television news anymore."

"Really? Why is that?"

"I'm not interested in their swaying opinions. I prefer to form my own opinion."

"Have they calmed down in DC this morning?"

"Somewhat. The demonstrators want national attention as they disrupt any event of their choosing. I wish there was a simple answer. This country is heading in the wrong direction. In fact, the entire world is acting stupid."

"Hold on."

"Server?"

"Yes sir."

"Will you turn that music down? All of a sudden it is blaring out at us."

"Sir, we're aware of it and attempting to regulate the volume. In fact, the manager turned it off and, it came right back on. Please bear with us."

"Okay, thanks."

The volume goes on up to a new level and then back down to very low. Then back up again.

"What is the problem with their music?"

The server returns to the table. "I am very sorry. We're trying to regulate the volume. This has never happened before and the manager is pulling her hair out in attempts to even completely turn it off."

Carl turns to Rufus, seated to his right and calls out, "Rufus!"

Benteson seems confused as he thinks. "Why is Carl scolding Rufus.? Did he do something?"

Rufus rolls his eyes to the left and away from the glare from Carl. He looks toward the hallway that leads to the kitchen. The music calms down.

Benteson asks. "What was that all about?"

"Rufus is always playing around and causing electronic disruptions, all in fun to him but, annoying to others. He is the culprit in this case."

"What?

He can do that? But he hasn't moved from his seat. How can he make changes to volume while sitting here?"

"Ask him."

"Rufus. I'm curious. How can you change the volume of music without moving from your chair?"

"Rufus can do that. Rufus has that ability."

"But, how?"

"That ability is beyond explanation and understanding of humans. You could not comprehend my electronic platform used for such a task."

Benteson looks over at Carl and shrugs his shoulders with a smile.

"Carl you and I have been around long enough to see the USA go downhill from when it was a great country. I see crap going on today that would have never been anticipated a few years ago, much less tolerated."

Rufus speaks up. "Rufus knows the solution."

Carl looks at Rufus. "Tell us about the solution you see for our country."

"Rufus knows it involves many other countries on the planet. The power struggle among leaders of countries that include America, Soviet Union, China, North Korea, Japan, Germany, Iran, Israel, all that have power goals."

"Carl and I understand that. So, what is the solution?"

"Rufus knows. The solution is Love. People have hatred toward others. People must learn to love each other. There is a deep-rooted cause that is growing with influence on susceptible individuals and introducing hatred. Once a person submits to that cause, they even begin to hate themselves. It's a form of depression."

Benteson says, "Please tell us more. You've hit a nerve and I'm curious."

First of all, people need to look at strangers and friends alike with kindness and love, to expect and see the good in their fellow man.

Carl asks, "Ok Rufus. And how in this world can we accomplish such an undertaking?"

Rufus responds, "I will explain the problem and the solution for people attending the scheduled conference. Unfortunately, humans do not possess sufficient intelligence to understand."

Carl tells Benteson, "I guess you and I will learn of Rufus's version for a solution at the Conference Center.

"Rufus, how do you know all this information and why do you believe in a solution?"

"Benteson, I can probably answer that. Rufus is linked to many computerized information and historical data systems, even indirectly to a few satellites. He is quite remarkable in everything he does. However, when communicating and offering human based solutions, Rufus has to hold back as he communicates on our level."

"Okay. Wow! I'm impressed, to say the least. Rufus, you have given me a lot of information to think about. Thank you!"

Rufus holds up his hand to speak and pauses for a moment. "There is a solution for you, each of you. I am still retrieving information. Later, I will tell you exactly what you can do and contribute toward a resolution for your country and its citizens."

Breakfast is delivered to the table. "Gentlemen, is there anything else I can provide."

Benteson responds. "No. Food looks appetizing. I would like some hot sauce, please."

"Yes sir."

"Carl, if my next question is out of line and none of my business, just ignore the inquiry. Okay?"

"Go ahead Benteson."

"How much did Rufus cost you?"

"LRC offers three versions of robots. LRC-1 is similar to a small file cabinet in size and appearance, basically stationary and immobile. It remains in one place, normally in a home or office. LRC-2 has full mobility and is intelligent. LRC-3 is as near human in appearance and actions as they can offer. Rufus is above that level and the only LRC-4 in existence. I paid one hundred forty thousand dollars for Rufus. That includes lifetime warranty, and guaranteed purchase price allowance toward any future sell up model."

"Oh my gosh! What if somebody kidnaps Rufus? What happens if he malfunctions, maybe turn against you?"

"There are terrific safeguards in place against any of those possibilities. Think about this. Rufus has quickly become a wholesome part of our family. He has no emotion of love for us as humans but, there is an element of care and certainty. That, within itself has tremendous value."

"I'm certain you enjoy Rufus and he seems content."

"Rufus enjoys Carl and Judy", says Rufus

Server approaches the table. "I'll leave the check with you. There is no rush. I have enjoyed serving you…and especially you, Rufus. I must leave early for court and a speeding ticket this morning." with a slight laugh.

Rufus quickly interrupts: "Tell Rufus about your speeding ticket."

Carl and Benteson remain quiet, wanting to see what Rufus is up to.

Carl tells the server, "It's okay. Share the details with Rufus."

"I was driving toward town on Buffalo Road. The speed was fifty-five. Then, it dropped to forty-five and later, on down to thirty-five. I was ticketed for driving fifteen miles per hour over the posted limit by a state trooper."

"And what is your name?"

"Mary Ann Bush."

"Rufus will go to court with you."

"Rufus! We need to go back home."

Rufus tells Mary Ann, "Carl will follow us to court and I will meet him after the hearing."

Carl admits being over ruled and goes along with Rufus's plan. "No. Rufus, you can ride with me. We'll follow Mary Ann to the courthouse."

Mary Ann is concerned and thinks, "This robot will get me in more trouble at court."

She responds, "Thanks, but I'll be okay. The fine will be no big deal for me."

"You gentlemen enjoy your breakfast and if you need anything, let me know. I'll check back with you in few minutes as I begin my check out, before leaving."

Carl hands her his credit card. "Go ahead and close us out. Add twenty percent for yourself."

"Wow. Thank you."

Carl is concerned. "Rufus, Mary Ann wants you to stay out of her court hearing."

"She needs me."

Benteson remarks, "As a group, we've been meeting for breakfast on a weekly basis for three or four years and none of us have ever had the slightest complaint. The service and food are always beyond expectations."

"I agree. Their chef is married to Stephanie at my store. She always has good things to say about him as a family man."

After their meal, Carl stands and slides his chair back in place. Rufus observes and does the same. Benteson leaves ahead of Carl and Rufus.

They walk toward the front of the restaurant and can hear conversation and laughter from a nearby table as they pass by.

"Hey buddy! Is that one of those weird mechanical boys tagging along with you there?"

Carl ignores the harsh tone as he and Rufus continue by the table with three younger men seated.

"Hey! I'm talking to you, old man!"

All three laugh. "He must be as dumb as that make believe boy. Neither one understands us."

Still no response from Carl as they continue walking.

One of the three men says. "Hey guys, come on let's follow them outside. We'll have some fun with that robot, or whatever it is."

As they rise from their chairs, each of their cell phones begins to ring at top volume, much louder than normal. Each guy stops and grabs their phone to answer with "hello."

In a very stern voice, they hear, "Cool it boys. Sit down! This is Rufus. Rufus likes you. Don't mess it up!"

Not another sound from the table as the three men look at each other, then watch as Rufus exits through the restaurant door. They return to their seats with a blank look about their face.

Carl smiles as they continue to the car. "That was pretty slick Rufus. I don't know what you did, exactly but you're a pro at handling situations."

Inside the car, they watch as Mary Ann backs out of a parking space and drives away. Carl follows her.

Traffic is calm during the ten-minute drive. At the courthouse, parking availability is limited as Mary Ann secures a spot on the west side of the building. Carl drove to another spot and parked. The three of them walk up the steps and through security to the court room.

Quietly seated, they observe as Judge Smith calls several cases, finding each guilty. The name Mary Ann Bush is then called. She rises and walks to the front.

"I am Mary Ann Bush."

"Mary Ann, you are charged with speeding. Trooper Dorning ticketed you for driving fifteen miles over the posted speed. How do you plead?"

Rufus stands nearby. "Your honor, I will represent Mary Ann. She pleads not guilty."

Judge Smith has a questioning facial expression. "I assume you are the artificially intelligent robot we have in our community. Are you an attorney?"

"My name is Rufus. I do not possess any license as an attorney. I do possess sufficient knowledge of the law in this state to adequately represent this lady. Judge Smith, I ask that you allow my presentation on behalf of Mary Ann Bush.

"This is very unusual. I am anxious to hear what you have to say. So, go ahead, Rufus."

"Your honor, Mary Ann was traveling into town on Buffalo Road and she met Trooper Dorning driving away from town. Dorning turned around and stopped Ms. Bush. He ticketed her for, specifically driving fifteen miles over the speed limit. She is here today to defend her citation."

"Okay Rufus. Go ahead. I believe this court is anxious to hear her defense."

"Yes, your honor. At the point of recording her speed, Ms. Bush had begun reducing her speed from the fifty-five limit to forty-five and on to thirty-five. Ms. Bush was driving fifty miles per hour in the forty-five zone just before it turned to thirty-five. Trooper Dorning assumed that she had already entered the thirty-five zone. She was eleven feet short of the lower limit. She was driving fifty miles per hour, still in the forty-five zone and, eleven feet short of the thirty-five zone. miles per hour over the posted speed limit of forty-five. Your honor, had she been in the thirty-five zone and driving fifty miles per hour, the citation would be correct. However, she was not driving fifteen mph over the forty-five posting.

"And, your honor, I have prepared some exact measurements of the distances involved for your consideration in this case."

"That is not necessary."

"Well, Trooper Dorning, its like an old saying. You have just been outwitted."

"This case is dismissed."

Mary Ann turns to Rufus. "Thank you, mister attorney robot!"

Rufus nods. "Are your returning to your job now?"

"Yes. Gotta make a living, you know."

Outside, she thanks Carl for allowing Rufus to help her as she walks toward her car.

"I need to stop by my jewelry store on our way home. You can go inside with me and I'll introduce you to everybody. However! You must not joke around and cause disruptions there. Okay?"

Rufus responds, "On the way to your business, we must stop at Miracle Eats again."

"Why? We were there earlier."

"It's important, very important. We must go there."

Carl thinks. "Okay."

The radio is tuned to a national talk show and top of the hour local news is discussing the early morning shooting across town. The shooter is still unknown. They are inside a local credit union with hostages. So far, nobody is known to be injured.

"That was the news you were talking about earlier today. Right Rufus? With your infinite wisdom, do you know any details? Do you know who the shooter was?"

"Rufus only knows there are two men holding hostages inside a credit union building."

Carl drives up to the restaurant front. He is still puzzled as to why Rufus feels the urgency to return.

"I want you to come inside with me, Carl."

"Why? Oh, okay, let's go inside."

"Carl, I want five hundred dollars, cash."

That request catches Carl off guard. "Why?"

"You always carry ten, hundred-dollar bills with you. I need five."

"I need to know what you're up to and, why do you think you need money?"

"Five, please. Go inside with me. You'll see the answer."

Carl reluctantly peels out five bills, each in one hundred dollars value.

"We'll enter now."

Inside, Rufus goes directly to a table and seats himself. Carl, still puzzled, joins him.

Mary Ann approaches. "Well look who is at this table, my favorite robot."

Carl remains still and calm as Rufus opens up to Mary Ann. "Carl would like a cup of coffee."

"Coming right up."

Mary Ann promptly serves coffee to Carl. Rufus thanks her.

"Okay. Rufus what are you up to? We're wasting time. I did not, and I do not want any coffee."

"You'll see. Are you now ready to leave?", asks Rufus.

"Why the heck not. I've acted stupidly through this whole scenario without having a clue as to what you are up to. So, let's get in the car and leave."

"I will pay for your coffee.", says Rufus.

No comment from Carl as they quickly exit the building. Outside, before opening the car drivers door, Carl stands facing Rufus.

"Now, bird brain, tell me what you have done, or what you are intending on doing with my money! You do not move until I know the answer."

Suddenly, the restaurant doors loudly slam open and startles Carl. Running toward the car, Mary Ann comes out crying and screaming at Rufus.

"Rufus! My darling, I love you! Oh my God, you are so, so wonderful", as she runs up to Rufus and wraps her arms around him.

Carl is still puzzled and stands motionless as he observes and wonders, "What is going on here?"

Finally, Mary Ann steps back, looking at Rufus. Then she turns to Carl. "Sir, thank you! Thank you so very much!"

Her emotions settle back down as Mary Ann kisses Rufus on the cheek and turns to walk back inside.

"Now, are you going to fill me in on what I just witnessed here?"

"Carl, Mary Ann is pregnant. She has very little money. You have provided her with renewed hope by leaving a five-hundred-dollar tip. You should pat yourself on the back. You performed a good deed for another human today."

Silence fills the vehicle as Carl drives toward the jewelry store.

CHAPTER 6

Entering the store parking lot and it appears the customer flow is good, based on the vehicles parked in front. Carl parks well out of the normal parking area to leave open spaces for customers to have easy access.

On the cell phone, Carl dials the store. "Sarah, I'm outside and our new robot, Rufus, is with me. Will you alert customers that we are about to enter the store? I don't want anybody to be concerned or upset because a robot is inside."

"Yes sir. I'll take care of it."

"Come on Rufus."

Rufus follows Carl to the store entrance. Carl opens the door and enters first. Only three customers are inside and all have completely stopped their shopping to observe this robot they have heard about on the news.

A couple approaches Carl. "We'd like to meet it. May we?"

"Yes. His name is Rufus."

"Rufus, my name is Kevin and this is my wife, Anna."

"Rufus likes you Kevin. Rufus likes you Anna. I hope you like me."

"Of course, we do." Says Anna. "You're adorable."

Others came over to meet Rufus and then everything begins to calm back down to normal. Carl goes in his office to retrieve any messages on his desk. One message is marked urgent from a pawn broker and Carl dials the phone number listed.

"Lou, this is Carl. I'm returning your call."

"Carl! Thanks for returning my call. I have an unusual diamond ring that I thought you would be interested in buying. I gave my customer a receipt for the ring so I can put a true value on it and he is to return at eleven o'clock this morning so I can make him an offer of purchase."

Lou describes the ring to Carl. "I know that ring! I sold it to a guy by the name of Randy as an engagement ring about two months ago and he has never paid me for it. Now, he is no longer engaged."

"You're right. His name is Randy. Randy Moresley."

"Tell you what, Lou. I'd like to be at your shop today when that guy arrives."

"Well, come on."

"I'm leaving my store right now. If you will hold on to the ring when he arrives, I'll walk in right after he does so you can have me look at the ring for a purpose of placing a value on it. I'll take it from there."

"That'll work for me."

Carl turns to Rufus. "Come on."

The drive across town is less than 15 minutes. Carl parks across the road from Lou's pawn shop. After less than ten minutes, a six-year-old corvette pulls up in front of the shop and Carl recognizes the young man as he gets out of the car and walks inside the shop. Carl slowly drives across the parking area and quietly eases his car up to the corvette rear bumper as a prevention in case the customer wants to leave with the merchandise. He instructs Rufus to remain in the car.

Lou calls out. "Carl, come on in. You're here just in time to help me put a value on this engagement ring for my customer."

Carl reaches out for the ring, looks it over carefully, and turns to Randy, then back to Lou.

He puts the ring in his shirt pocket. "Lou, this is my ring. This young man is Randy Mosley and he has never paid me for the ring."

"You're crazy! That is my ring! I bought that ring from a friend!"

"Lou, Randy bought this ring for his girlfriend. I believe her name was Jackie. She came by my store after she broke up with Randy and wanted to let me know that he kept the ring. My ring is now in my pocket and its going back to my jewelry store."

"I'm calling the police! You are trying to steal my ring!"

"Go ahead. Back at my store is all the documentation with your signature on it. So, call the police. The ring is going with me."

Randy slams his fist down on the counter and turns to Carl. "That is your car blocking my corvette!"

He bursts out the shop door and gets in his car to back out, intending on pushing Carl's car all the way into the road and among ongoing traffic. He turns the key in the ignition. Nothing happens. After several attempts, he sees Carl standing in front of the car with his arms folded. He gradually strolls along the driver side of Randy's car to his own vehicle.

Carl opens his door, gets in the car and turns to Rufus with a high five, while knowing he must have electronically disabled Randy's car. He slowly backs away from the corvette, pulls up alongside Randy, rolls the passenger window down and tells Randy. "Mr. Morsley, your car will now start as it should. Have a nice afternoon."

Randy, very upset, continues to stare straight forward with both hands on the steering wheel as if to ignore Carl.

"Rufus, I continue to be amazed. It is beyond my comprehension with your ability to establish contact and change or disable electronics without any physical contact."

"Rufus can do things."

"I know that! But I wonder how you do it and, I know your explanation is probably well beyond my ability to understand. So, we'll just leave it at that."

"May I sing while you drive?"

With a laugh, "Rufus, your voice is flat and very monotone. I don't believe you can sing very well."

"I can sing just like Lisa Presley."

"Lisa Marie Presley doesn't sing. Elvis Presley was a singer."

"At least I now know that you are paying attention to me. Listen. You ain't nothin' but a hound dawg, just a barkin' all the time."

"Rufus! Rufus! Come on. Knock it off! You're not a singer! Okay? You may be an entertainer in your own unusual way, but you are not a singer."

"I'll talk to you about my uncle."

"Rufus, you have no relatives. You're a robot. Sometimes, an intelligent robot."

"Without uncle Sam I would never have been here today."

"Uncle Sam? Who is uncle Sam?"

"Oh brother. Uncle Sam as in the head of the United States many years ago. Uncle Sam is responsible for me being here."

Silence.

Carl drives to, and parks his car in an open space alongside his jewelry store. Inside the store Carl walks directly to his general manager, Julie. "This is a repossessed engagement ring we have retrieved from Randy Mosely. Clean it up and price it at thirty-three ninety-five."

"I'll take care of it right now. Did you have any trouble getting the ring back from the guy? He attempted to rip us off, wasn't he?"

"No trouble at all. I do want to do something for Lou because without his involvement we would have lost the ring and the dollars involved. Let's send him a gift for his wife. How about a dinner gift certificate for two hundred dollars, in the form of a pre-paid credit card so they can eat at any restaurant they want."

"Yes sir."

"Oops! Now where the heck is Rufus?"

Julie responds, "Oh, he's standing over there, to the right."

"Okay, I see him. Rufus? Are you ready to go?"

"Rufus is ready."

Carl walks toward the store front door. Rufus remains in place. "Rufus. Come on."

Rufus is still not moving.

Carl turns and takes a couple of steps toward Rufus. "What's up? What are you doing, Rufus?" "Why are you patting your foot like that? Rufus! Let's go."

"Rufus is being entertained at the moment."

Oh no. Now what? "Rufus Let's go."

By now, everybody in the store is paying attention and wondering what's going on with this robot.

"Now, Rufus will go with you."

Carl thinks. "I won't even go there. There is no telling what this high-level peon was up to, standing over against the wall and patting his foot."

At home, Judy greets Carl and Rufus. "How was breakfast with the group?"

"Benteson was the only one there. The other two were absent for various reasons. But we enjoyed the get together. Rufus laid out some fundamentals that hangs over America and is responsible for changing life as we know it here."

"Really? So, does Rufus favor the liberal or conservative agenda?"

"Amazingly, neither yet, both, if that makes sense. But what he had to tell Benteson and me was fresh information and right on target and absent of any emotion toward politics. Basically, human beings are in trouble if we continue on the current path. He says he knows what we can do about all the crap going on in this country and he'll tell us in an upcoming conference."

"I can't wait."

"Here is a highlight of the morning. Rufus volunteered to appear in court and help our waitress get her speeding ticket thrown out."

"How'd he do that?"

"Don't ask. It was part of his being the world's greatest legal intelligence."

Carl turns and calls out. "Rufus? Where's Rufus? Hey, Rufus. I can use your help. Where are you?"

"Judy, do you know where Rufus is?"

"No."

Carl walks throughout the house then to the back yard as he looks for Rufus. "This is ridiculous. Where can he be?" thinks Carl.

With all other areas searched, Carl walks out to the garage.

"Rufus! What in the world do you think you are doing? Why are you sitting in the driver seat of my car?"

"Rufus has now engaged in operating this vehicle. Rufus can now drive this vehicle."

"I don't think so! Get out of the car! You need to come with me. I need your assistance. Now!"

Rufus recognizes Carl's harsh voice as, "I guess he means it", and exits the car to follow Carl through the house and out to the back yard.

"You and I need to move that huge oak tree section that has been cut into manageable section. It's still too heavy for me to lift. Do you think the two of us can move it?"

No response as the two of them make their way out to the partial tree trunk. Carl grasps beneath the heavier end of the trunk and tells Rufus to help with the lighter end.

Rufus made some quick calculations and starts back toward the house.

"Rufus! Where are you going? Come back here and help!"

Rufus stops. Turning back to Carl. "Are you really that naive?"

"Naive? I want to move the tree trunk! Get back here and help!" Rufus returns to help with the tree. "You are not capable of managing the heavier end. I am available to do that. You must grip the lighter end and Rufus will oversee placement of the tree trunk."

The two of them easily maneuver the tree trunk to a new location, one that is not noticeable from the house. "Okay Rufus, this will make Judy happy. She was tired of seeing that tree trunk each time she walked out on the deck."

"Rufus, sometimes you are too smart for your britches."

"These are not Rufus's britches. These are your hand-me-down britches. You are a larger man.

These trousers that you are calling britches are almost too large for Rufus".

"Whatever."

Back inside the house, Carl tells Judy. "I'm going back to the store for a couple of hours. Sarah has an appointment with her doctor and I should be available to the staff."

"Okay. Harper and Mollie will be over at 6:30."

"That's good. Rather than take meat from the freezer, I can stop by the Publix market and pick up four filet mignons. Do we have sweet potatoes?"

"No. And we need a fresh garden salad mix."

"Anything else?"

"Not that I can think of. I'll call you if I think of anything else."

"Okay. I'll be back by four-thirty. Rufus will stay here."

"Okay. Bye hon."

Rufus eases his way back toward the deck.

"I would like to talk with you, Rufus. Let's sit outside. Okay?"

"Rufus enjoys the outdoors."

"You heard Carl and me as we prepared for having Mollie and Harper Pinkelbrooke over for a cookout, didn't you?"

"Rufus heard."

"You will enjoy Mollie and Harper. They're nice people."

Judy sets back and relaxes as she looks out over the back yard and wooded area.

"Rufus, are you comfortable living here with Carl and me?"

"Rufus is here to please you and Carl. It is not for me to determine whether I am comfortable or not comfortable. You are asking me a question that applies to emotions and Rufus has no emotions."

"You are right. I forget that sometimes. You are so much of a pleasure that it's easy for us to forget that you are not human."

"Incoming call and Judy steps inside the house to answer. "Hello."

"Judy, this is Mollie. What can I bring as a side dish this evening?"

"We've got about everything we need. How about some sautéed mushrooms? I remember you have a special recipe and they were delicious."

"Mushrooms it is. What time should we be at your house?"

"Around six thirty will be a good time. Carl is going to grill steaks on the charcoal grill. Normally he fires up the gas grill but, charcoal seems to add flavor to steaks."

"That sounds great. We'll see you at six thirty.

"We're looking forward to it."

Judy turns to observe Rufus from inside. She wishes Carl were there to see this magnificent show. Rufus has seven beautiful birds on and near him. A squirrel nears Rufus.

Judy whispers. "This is absolutely amazing. Nothing else attracts creatures like Rufus. He has no emotions to attract another live being, no attracting odor, nothing that makes sense. However, critters seem to adore him. Animals apparently see him as non-threatening. But, why do they come to him? Animals would have no way of receiving any of his electronic communications. Or can they? Oh well. I'll leave them be and get the house in order for guests this evening."

As Judy spot cleans areas of the kitchen, she periodically glances at Rufus as the birds and animals enjoy his presence.

She decides to call their veterinarian friend, Dr. Bishop.

"Jimmy, this is Judy Forecrast."

"Hey there."

"Jimmy, you know that we have a robot living with us, don't you?"

"Come to think of it, I have heard about it."

"He is lovely. He has no emotions, of course, which leads me to the reason for this call."

Laughing, "I was beginning to wonder why you're calling a veterinarian to treat a robot"

"Jimmy, our robot attracts birds, vicious dogs, and other animals to him. They seem to adore being around him. What can be the attraction?"

Hmmmm. "I have medical no answer for that attraction. If I had to guess, I would say that your robot has the ability to give off a signal, probably a high-pitched sound that humans can't hear but animals do hear and are attracted to the noise. Animals may not be threatened by the robot and they find comfort in the sound he is able to transmit."

"I may want to call later on and visit to observe the robot. May I do so?"

"Yes. Just call us."

"Okay. I'll look forward to it. And this may be good information for a veterinary manual. Take care. I'll call you."

Returning to the family room for a view of Rufus and the animals, Rufus is nowhere in sight.

Judy steps onto the deck, looking all around.

"Rufus!"

"Rufus? Rufus, where are you? Rufus answer me."

No response.

Judy is now in a panic. Where is Rufus? She hurriedly runs around to the front of their house and looks.

"Rufus?"

To the back yard again, she runs toward the wooded area at the back of their property.

"Rufus? Rufus! Answer me. Where are you?"

Now, with a long sigh, she sees Rufus emerging through some tall bushes as he walks toward her.

"Rufus, I was worried about you. What were you doing in those woods?"

Then she sees he is carrying something in his arms and being followed by a deer.

"This fawn was dying from lack of food. Its mother was not allowing the baby deer to get nourishments from her milk. Rufus calmed her and she allowed some feeding. Her baby is very weak and near lifeless. Rufus will continue to care for both the mother and her baby for twenty-one hours."

Judy has questions ramping through her mind. "Where is he going to care for these animals? Not inside my home, for sure. Why twenty-one hours?"

"Rufus, I admire you for the care you're offering the fawn and its mother. I would ask how you persuaded the mother to allow her fawn to finally get nourishment, but I probably would not understand."

"I'll rush in the house for a blanket to lay the fawn on."

"No. Rufus will place the baby near its mother on the grassy area near the deck. Human scents on the blanket would dramatize the mother and discourage it from providing milk to the fawn."

"You need to distance yourself from both as the mother is very uncomfortable knowing a human is nearby."

"Okay. I'll step inside the house and watch."

Rufus lays the fawn on the grass as the doe watches. He then rushes to the bushes and brings an arm load of leafy limbs to place high around the fawn. He wants the baby deer to be amidst familiar surroundings and feel safe from any possible intruders.

Judy remains very quiet and motionless in amazement and admiration for all that is going on. Rufus then joins her and looks over the fawn laying with its mother. No obvious anxiety with either.

After Rufus is satisfied, he joins Judy inside the house.

Judy's admiration remains elevated as she finds comfort in Rufus's amazing care for other beings, yet with his lack of emotions.

As the afternoon goes on, Rufus keeps a watchful eye on the doe and fawn.

At fifteen minutes after four, Carl walks in. "Hi hon."

"Carl! Come here. Quickly!"

"What's wrong?"

"No. You've got to see this! Rufus brought that small fawn and the doe to deck area. The baby appears so frail and under-nourished."

Why is that? Do you think the mother is not feeding her baby? What is Rufus going to do?"

"Rufus must have found that fawn and doe in those woods. I'm assuming the doe would not allow the fawn any milk and Rufus did something to persuade her to feed the baby. He then brought both up here so he can care for them twenty-one hours"

"Really? Why twenty-one hours?"

"Who knows. It may have something to do with the multiple of sevens that Rufus knows about."

Carl shrugs his shoulders as he accepts the actions of Rufus.

"Rufus. You are amazing. We take pride in having you as part of our family."

"Rufus enjoys being with you and Judy. You have guests coming to visit. Rufus will continue to observe the deer and fawn over the next twenty-one hours until the baby is healthy. You may prepare for the guest's visit."

Judy follows up to Carl. "You're just in time. Our guests will be here soon. Beyond your steaks, everything is ready."

"Okay, Judy. I'm going get the grill ready and then I will take a quick shower."

"Rufus, the doe and fawn are out back, not too close to the grill, but do you think they will be disturbed by my cooking."

"Rufus will go out with you as you approach your grill. Rufus will calm the mother and baby. You may be able to continue with your grilling."

"No. Let them be. I will use a portable grill in another area."

"Rufus, you're very special."

"I know that."

"Yeah. Right."

Carl's cell phone rings. Carl does not recognize the number. "Hello."

"Mr. Forcrast, my name is Jody Hamp with WB news. You're the talk of the area. I understand you now own a robot, apparently a very intelligent robot. I and our camera crew would like to video a segment about you and the robot, preferably at your home. Will you allow us to do that?"

"Okay. The robot's name is Rufus, spelled R u f u s. I am Carl and my wife is Judy. When?"

"Can we come out to you tomorrow afternoon, say around three o'clock?"

"Three o'clock it is. Do you have the address?"

"Yes. We'll see you then. I hope you have a wonderful evening."

CHAPTER 7

At five forty, the doorbell sounds and Judy says. "That must be Molly and Harper."

Carl opens the door and welcomes the guests. "Harper, it's good to see you. Molly, I'd like a hug. You folks come on in."

Molly responds with a thank you as she turns toward Judy. "Look how pretty you are this afternoon. You've done something with your hair. I like it."

"I had it cut. That's all"

"Well, it looks great."

"Come on in. We can hang out in the family room for a while."

Carl opens the conversation. "You know about our robot, Rufus, don't you?"

"Yes. You told us about it and we have also heard some information from the Sawyers'."

"Well, if you glance outside, Rufus has become the temporary caretaker for a doe and its fawn."

"Do what? Do you mean....I mean....how can that deer and little one stay this close to your house?"

"Only Rufus knows that. We believe he has the ability to send out a high frequency sound that calms and attracts animals to him."

"We would like to meet Rufus. Can we do that?"

"Sure."

Carl gently cracks open patio door and whispers, "Rufus... Rufus? Come inside and meet our guests."

Rufus walks back inside and approaches Mollie. "I am Rufus. I like you. I hope you like me."

He then turns to Harper. "I am Rufus. I like you. I hope you like me."

"Oh yes. We like you already." Says Mollie.

Harper questions Rufus, "I have heard that robots like you are many times more intelligent than humans. Is that true? And, from where do you get such intelligence?"

"Rufus knows. Rufus obtains information and data from many available sources, even from selected systems that communicate with satellites."

"Wow!"

Harper turns to Carl. "He connects to satellites?"

"Rufus, will you explain your satellite connections to Harper?"

"Rufus does not have direct contact to some satellites, only through their ground bases. Basically, all satellites send information to its individual command center. Rufus can link electronically to certain command centers."

Carl speaks up. "Beyond that ability, Rufus can connect with all electronic human history, medical, political, legal information and files to further expand his higher level of intelligence. Human beings do not have the ability to learn and store all the information that Rufus easily possesses."

Mollie cringes. "Oh my gosh. That's great. No, it's scary."

Rufus excuses himself as he makes his way to the rear door and studies the mother and baby, as he prefers to call them. He wants to make certain the small fawn is nourished and both are resting. Satisfied with the pair, Rufus returns to Carl, Judy, and guests.

Harper share the recent news, "The morning news about the shooting was horrible. Our politicians have got to pull all guns and prevent future killings in this country. I can't believe we're allowing people to possess weapons."

Carl responds. "I agree that we need to stop the killings. I do not believe taking away guns will solve the problem. Guns don't kill people, people kill people."

"That's crazy! If people have no guns, people would not be murdered!"

"But Harper, listen to me for a minute. If we pull the guns from legitimate, registered owners that possess a gun for hunting or protection, only the those with ill intent will use their guns as they rob, break into your home, and whatever they want to do. Then people like you and I will have no means of protection against the ill-fated person holding a gun on our family as they rob and murder us."

"That's why government needs to pull all guns. All guns! If nobody has a gun, police would have little reason to go after robbers and thieves and could simply arrest a thief and allow courts to deal with them".

"Sounds good on the surface. However, regardless of any laws to apprehend all weapons, the criminal along with the youngster with a pistol, they will not give up their gun. That's a fact. So, I guess you and I agree to disagree on that subject. That will be a good topic for Rufus to share with us."

"As Mollie may have told you, we're having steak for dinner. I really don't want to bother the deer. So, instead of cooking out back, I have a small portable charcoal grill near the garage that will work well. Come on Harper, walk out with me. We can talk while I start the charcoals."

In the garage, Carl makes his way around their two vehicles, pulls out the small grill, some charcoal and lighter, and sets the grill up outside. Spreading charcoal evenly in the grill he then sprays some fluid over the surfaces.

"I usually allow the fluid to soak in for about three minutes before lighting the chunks."

"I remember the delicious foods you always cook, whether it's on your gas grill or this charcoal grill. So, I always pay attention and learn from you." Says Harper.

"Carl, you have a beautiful place out here. How much property do you own?"

"There is only a couple of acres of land. We enjoy the quiet life style out here in the county."

Rufus quietly walks up and listens.

"Do you have any crime out here? asks Harper.

"None. Generally, our neighbors park their vehicles inside their garage. About eight years ago somebody came through the area looking for cars parked outside the homes, checking for unlocked doors and they helped themselves to a few contents. A neighbor had them on his outdoor security cameras so, they were apprehended almost immediately."

"How would Rufus respond to a thief?"

"Rufus. What would you do in case of a threat or break in?"

"Rufus knows what to do. Rufus would react appropriately to protect innocent humans and their properties."

"But, how would you react?"

"Rufus is programmed to respond effectively. How Rufus would respond would depend on the need."

"Oh, okay."

Harper laughs. "I guess you'll know the answer to that when and if it happens."

"I guess so. While the coals are heating up more, I'll get the steaks. I'll be right back."

"Okay."

Harper turns to Rufus. "Rufus, can you fire a gun, and have you ever shot a gun?".

"Yes. Rufus can accurately fire a gun. Rufus has never done that."

"By your response, I can tell that you don't like guns. Right?"

"Firearms can be good. Firearms can be used for food. Some people use firearms as a horrible weapon against innocent people."

"So, you agree with me. The government should pull away all weapons from people."

"Rufus knows that is not the solution. Government must not take weapons from law abiding citizens. And, it would be in violation of your constitution that is legally binding on Americans."

"Okay Mr. smart guy. As a robot with all your assumed intelligence, what is your non-human solution?"

"Love."

"Love? Now, you've set out on a new course. Explain to me how love will replace guns."

"Love will not replace weapons. Love will limit them to their intended use, not murdering humans."

"Humans have hatred for each other. Countries have hatred for other countries. Convert all the hatred to love and the problem is solved."

"Ha. That's never going to happen! And you must know that. So, in my opinion, we're back to taking away all firearms."

"Without guns to assume protection against murdering, killers would still kill other humans as they revert to using knives, arrows, and other means of killing. If a killer wants to murder, they don't need a gun to do so."

Carl walks up with four nice filet mignons on a tray, well covered to protect them, still waiting on the coals to be hotter.

"You and Rufus have enjoyed getting to know each other while I was inside?"

"Yeah. Rufus wants everybody on the planet to love each other. That's not going to take place."

Carl responds. "Sounds like a good approach to me."

"I guess in theory, he may have the right solution but, we're in the real world and people are people. Can you imagine that killer, Charles Manson, loving somebody, or being loved? Anybody! And there are thousands on this planet like him. They are not capable of love."

"Rufus? What is your response to that?"

"Rufus knows. That statement is inaccurate. People can learn to love each other."

Harper responds. "You really don't think our politicians can love their country and the people rather than themselves, do you?"

Carl speaks up. "Let me answer that for you. If leaders did love the people and people loved the politicians, can you imagine how effective and smoothly our country would be governed?'

"Carl, you're surely familiar with all the loopholes associated with the word "if", are you not?"

"I am. Rufus, what do you have to say?"

"Elected government decision makers in Washington are influenced and intimated by an overall system that is managed by nine super powerful people from many parts of the planet." Elected politicians become ineffective beginning with their initial winning of an election. Politicians set an example that many people tend to lean on. If your politicians showed love, were truthful, and did not set out to improperly and illegally acquire millions of dollars while in office, their example of love would then become a national way of life. If voters based their vote on the sincerity of the politician that began and ended every speech, every campaign, with a prayer. Think about the change and influence that would quickly begin taking place in America. Within twenty-three years, the greatness of America would return. Hatred would fade from most, not all, as you say but, most. Love for others would become the enjoyable way of life. People would help the fellow man to become financially secure and love."

"Instead, they are seen as lying, cheating, and corruptors, which are the means that seem to self-satisfy toward their personal goals."

Harper is looking off as he thinks about church and love. He then turns to Rufus. "Rufus, Carl, I had never looked at our world problems from that angle. Interesting. Very interesting, I must say. However, it will never work."

"Okay guys, our steaks are ready. Judy has the other food ready for us so, let's go inside."

Rufus leans over for a better look at the steaks. "Carl, my steak is far too rare."

"Then, grab a can of that 10w 30w engine oil from this shelf and enjoy it."

As Carl covers the grill and starts inside, Harper says. "Rufus, after we eat, I want to hear more about your version of our political system and that silly stuff about love as our solution."

Mollie eyes the thick steaks. "Oh, my goodness! Those steaks look and smell delicious. I can hardly wait."

Judy responds. "Wait until you bite into yours. Carl uses a kitchen tenderizing chopper that punches very small holes throughout the meat and then, he covers it with a mixture of a small portion of his own sauce. After it soaks into the meat, he rubs virgin olive oil over the outside and grills it over very hot fire."

Carl laughs. "Judy, you're giving away my secrets."

Judy reaches out to hold Carl's hand. "Hon, will you offer the blessing?"

"Absolutely."

After the prayer, the salad, bread, and vegetables are passed around the table.

Harper speaks up. "So, Rufus, continue with your ideas about guns and government."

We're all interested in hearing how you think we can make it happen."

"Harper, I may have a better way to work through this topic and others that you will be anxious to hear. Rufus is gaining a reputation for his knowledge throughout the area and has been asked speak to a group at the old gymnasium building on Willow road. Why don't join us there? You may bring a list and introduce the topics so others can hear his answer. Will that be okay?"

"Sure. That may be better and I can hardly wait. For some reason, I already have respect for any answer Rufus may offer."

"I'll call you as soon as the meeting is firmly scheduled."

Mollie comments, "Harper, that sounds good to me. That way we can keep this visit informal in our discussions. Too much political conversation can be negative."

As they enjoy dinner, conversations continue.

Harper asks. "Carl have you all been traveling lately?"

"Not recently. We have a bucket list of travels and now we will want to include Rufus. He is always a pleasure to have with us and, sometimes accounts for some unusual excitement. Ha!"

"Mollie and I are planning a trip to Jackson Hole, Wyoming in January"

"Jackson Hole is a great place to visit, especially in the winter when they have lots of snow to enjoy."

"Oh. You've been there. I forgot about that. And you enjoyed it?"

"We sure did. A highlight of our trip was hiring a guide and renting snow mobiles. The guide led us far up in the mountains and to a log cabin. He unpacked our lunch of soup and sandwiches from a huge ice type chest he had been pulling behind his lead mobile. After lunch, we relaxed for a bit. During the tour, we encountered cougar, elk, fox, and other animals from a distance. You'll enjoy Jackson Hole."

"Carl, that was absolutely the best steak I have ever eaten. You should open a restaurant." Says Harper.

"Oh no. I've got enough responsibility now without expanding to another venture."

Throughout the evening discussions about travels, food, and Rufus continue until well into the hours. Rufus remains quiet as he listens to a variety of discussions while remaining attentive and periodically checks on the fawn.

"Carl and Judy, it's getting late and we should be on our way."

"Do you really need to leave now? Asks Judy."

"Yes. We need to go home and check on our new puppy. He is good at holding it for up to about 5 hours and, we're approaching four hours now."

Everybody bids good evening as Harper and Mollie walk out the door and toward their car. Carl walks out part way and waves as they are seated, and walks back inside.

Almost immediately, Harper is back at the door, ringing the doorbell.

"Hey Carl, do you have some battery cables? My car won't start."

"I'll be right out."

"Rufus. You're an electronic whiz. How about helping us determine why his car won't start?"

Standing by the car, Rufus looks at Carl, then to Harper.

"Your car engine will start now."

"What? But we didn't do anything." Says Harper.

"Harper, the car will start now."

Harper turns on the ignition to find that his car starts right up.

"Harper, I apologize. Rufus is up to his electronic genius mischief again."

Rufus replies. "Rufus just wanted them to understand that they are welcome to visit for a while longer in spite of their urges to leave."

Mollie laughs. "Rufus! You're a hoot. For certain."

Back inside the house, Judy asks Rufus if he enjoyed their visit.

"Rufus liked Mollie and Harper. They do not sincerely believe there is a Greater Being and, they have some weird tendencies. Yet, they are enjoyable to be with."

"Some people are uninformed. Some are just mis-informed and not reaching for accurate information. We attended church a few times and just got out of the habit of going. Rufus, your statement to me about God grabbed my attention, especially coming from your level intelligence."

Judy says. "Carl, you never told me about a conversation with Rufus about God."

"Recently, while we were sitting outside, Rufus told me directly, *There is a greater being, you call Him God. You need to pay attention.* and that statement hit me hard. Judy, we need to attend church again and learn about God."

"I'm glad to hear you say that, Carl. Let's commit to attend-ing a church."

"Rufus, we're going to bed. Enjoy your night and we'll see you in the morning."

"Rufus will see you when you rise tomorrow morning."

Next morning and everybody moves about as normal. Rufus remains quiet while he observes Judy delivering coffee to Carl and then continues by making a fresh cup for herself.

Carl walks through the dining area and to the kitchen. He sees Rufus standing, "Good morning smart boy."

"Smart boy? How about most intelligent highness to you, you overweight dude?"

"Overweight? Overweight? I am only 17 pounds above the recommended weight for my height."

"Like Rufus said. "Overweight."

Carl laughs. "Judy, I've got a chamber of commerce meeting this morning. Will you pull this underweight thing back in line while I'm gone?"

"Oh, get out of here. Have a good meeting and I'll see you later."

Judy and Carl kiss and Carl walks away then stops. "Oh, I forgot, the local tv station is going to be here at four o'clock for an interview with the three of us as they make a news report about our wonderful Mr. smart Rufus."

"We'll be ready."

"Rufus knows that Carl is overweight. Don't you agree, Judy?"

"I'm not venturing to that discussion. I'm going to sit down and relax for a while."

"Rufus will join you. Rufus will answer your questions."

"I have no questions of you at this time."

"Really? Do you know Carl's twin brother, Cramer?"

"I do. He lived in Dallas for many years and moved back here three years ago. We don't see him very often."

"Rufus knows much about Cramer. Cramer was married to Lucy first for only seven weeks and that marriage was annulled."

"You know too much! Some things should be kept to yourself. What you are saying is recognized as gossip."

"Rufus knows. Rufus knows that Lucy gave birth to a child and Cramer is unaware of that child."

"Rufus! Don't you dare go there! Stop it! If that is true, Carl and I do not need or want to know about it! Keep other people's personal lives to yourself!"

"Rufus will not gossip about Cramer."

"I'm going to take a nap." Says Judy.

Rufus observes as Judy leans back in the recliner and closes her eyes. He remains standing as his round eyes, somewhat larger than human eyes, looks around the room and out through the patio doors. The doe and fawn are still in place outside the house. He knows they will leave and return to the woods and their established environment soon.

Rufus is whizzing through things he can do to impress Carl and Judy.

"Aha!" thinks Rufus. "I will prepare a homemade banana pudding from a 1948 version of a Watkins cookbook" That book belonged to Carl's grandmother at one time. In the mid-twentieth century, Watkins distributors would go door-to-door selling the Watkins brand of flavorings, herbs, and other cooking compliments to households. The J. R. Watkins cookbooks were a big hit in earlier days. So, Rufus pulls up the recipe from his database and quietly goes about surprising Carl and Judy with a desert.

He locates the flour, salt, eggs, milk, quickly. His search for bananas and vanilla wafers took him searching through the backup food pantry near the utility room. First, he cut the bananas into small sections and placed them in a bowl for access later. He then mixed an exact portion of milk, egg yolk, and four in a double boiler and brought it to a boil, steering constantly to avoid sticking. Once the mixture was ready, he began layering wafers on the bottom of the pan, topped with banana slices and then, he poured some mixture. Placing more wafers and banana slices in the pan continued until four layers were completed. Next, he mixed the egg whites and sugar to form a thick meringue which was then spread all across the top of the pan contents. The oven was pre-set to 350 degrees and ready for the mixture. Rufus watched the pudding mixture and meringue until small heat related areas appeared on top and he removed it from the oven.

"Perfecto" he thought.

"Carl and Judy will enjoy real home-made banana pudding."

CHAPTER 8

Judy is still dozing. Carl has not yet returned home. Rufus looks around for anything he can do as amusement. Leisurely, he walks throughout the house and ends up in Carl's closet. Browsing through the clothes, he selects a pair of levi jeans and examines the size. It appears the length is close, about two inches shorter than his existing size. He decides to try them on. The waist is by far too large. After all these pants have fit fat boy Carl perfectly. He looks for a belt and instead grabs a necktie and ties it around the waistline to hold the pants in place. He spots an old shirt that Carl has had from years ago and slides his arms into each sleeve, buttons up the front, leaving the top three buttons open, turns up the cuff on each arm and then flips up the collar at his neck. "I'm Elvis Presley.?" Rufus thinks.

He hears Carl enter from the garage and is greeted by Judy as the doorbell rings. Carl proceeds to the door and opens it to see the television crew standing outside. "Come on in. I'm Carl and this is Judy."

"My name is Billy Brantley with TV6. This is our camera person, Tamika".

"A pleasure meeting you. We can go into the living room for this session if that is ok with you, Billy."

"Absolutely."

"Judy, were is Rufus?"

"He should be inside somewhere,"

"Rufus? Rufus, where are you? Come on in the living room. The television station crew is here and wants to meet you."

From the master suite area adjoining the living room Rufus jumps through the doorway as he imitates holding a guitar, and sings "You ain't nothin' but a hound dog" as he swings his hips. Then he says. "Thank you. Thank you very much."

Everybody cracks up laughing.

After the laughing calms down, "That is a hilarious entry." Says Billy.

"Rufus, you are an embarrassment. What in the world have you been up to? What are you doing in all that garb?"

"Billy, Rufus is extremely smart but, he has no common sense. No horse sense as we called it when I was a youngster."

Rufus ignores Carl and walks over to Billy. "My name is Rufus. I like you. I hope you like me."

Billy is amazed and thinks. "This is all caught on camera and is going to make a hit for our station."

Billy then makes a suggestion. "Rufus, why don't you sit in that chair and face the camera."

Rufus seats himself in the chair and turns slightly toward the camera and crew. Billy continues with some instructions.

"Now, Carl and Judy, please be seated on the sofa. Just take a couple of deep breaths and relax."

All seated, Billy announces to the camera. "We are in the home of Carl and Judy Forcrast along with Rufus. Rufus is the first artificially intelligent robot in our area. We're privileged to be a part of this historical time."

Carl, Judy, and Rufus acknowledge the introduction with a nod.

"Carl, I know you enjoy having Rufus as part of your family. Was it as simple as it seems in the adoption process of bringing him to your home and indoctrinating him to the environment?"

"It was indeed. Rufus, to us is not a computerized mechanical thing, or "it". He is addressed and enjoyed as if he were a person. We refer to Rufus as "He", not "it". He is part of our family, and a indeed a pleasure."

"Rufus, do you enjoy the Forcrast family and the acceptance into their home."

"Rufus does enjoy Carl and Judy. Judy is smarter than Carl. Carl thinks he is ruler of the house but, he's just not intelligent enough to understand his role as Judy's assistant."

Everybody giggles.

Carl fires back with, "Like I said, Rufus has no common sense."

The camera then catches Rufus looking straight to the camera lens. With his left arm extended, he points to Carl. His right hand then makes a circling motion with his index finger toward his right ear, indicating his opinion of Carl's lack of intelligence.

Again, the camera crew giggles. While Carl and Judy were looking at the camera, they are in the dark as to why all the laughter.

Billy continues, "Rufus, how are you smarter than geniuses? Tell us how that can be."

"Rufus knows but, Rufus can't explain it to you in terms that you would comprehend and even vaguely understand. Rufus can access all worldwide historical data, indirectly to some satellites, communications, medical and legal information that may include some Government data."

"Government data?" So, you can tell us about underlying secrets of the United States and, even other countries? Tell us an example."

"Rufus is programmed to withhold government secrets and knowledge that could affect, even alter future beyond your current understanding."

"How about unidentified flying objects and extraterrestrial explorations?"

"Rufus will share his knowledge about other beings in our universe at a later time and date."

"Really? Wow. So, what you are saying is there are other beings in our solar system?"

"Your solar system is huge with earth and other planets rotating around its sun. And, the vast universe has many solar systems, each with planets rotating around their own sun. Other beings, some human type, and other species do exist, they are your God's beings also."

"Now you have really got my interest. Is that why the United States is venturing out in search of other intelligence?"

"Absolutely. However, world governments are tight lipped about findings. Other intelligence will be announced someday."

"Okay. Rufus, what is the world peace and total happiness solution?"

"Your entire globe with friendly, happy people of all races and cultures will be discussed later when you have had a chance to absorb and understand some of the more complexities that I will discuss in detail later on, on another day. You will be invited to attend that conference."

Carl speaks up. "Billy, do you have an extra few minute in this interview, fifteen minutes to observe something you have never seen before?"

"We do. What do you have in mind?"

"Okay, everybody come with me to the den. Bring your camera."

Carl leads the way followed by Billy and the crew, then Rufus and Judy. Turning to Rufus, "Rufus why don't you walk out on the deck and invite your friends over."

Cameras are set up to record the invitation. Billy and the crew are somewhat in suspense because they have no idea what to expect. Carl instructs everybody remain quiet and still as they observe Rufus and the area.

A hawk is spotted circling and swooping down from a nearby tree to tree. A wild turkey and three chicks stroll across the yard about seventy feet away and to the left, keeping a distance from the activity. "That's unusual but no big deal." thinks Billy.

Tamika whispers. "Oh my gosh! Isn't that a fox near the brush? It is! It is a fox. Wow!"

"And, look at that baby deer, the little fawn!" says Billy.

As they remain calm and observant, the fawn, and squirrel make their way toward Rufus. As they near him, the hawk dives down from a nearby tree and lands on Rufus's left forearm.

Seemingly protective of her young, the doe quickly emerges from the wooded area and trots toward her fawn.

Billy whispers. "I have never heard of animals of any kind being so drawn to anybody or anything without regard for the normal fear of each other."

Tamika becomes emotional and begins to softly whimper. This is not possible, she thinks. She turns to Billy and whispers. "We're recording this. That is precious. Amazing!"

Judy reaches for a tissue and hands it to Tamika and whispers, "It's okay Tamika. What we're seeing here illustrates purity in animal love and emotions."

Carl whispers to Billy and Tamika. "I wish you could have been here to witness an injured raccoon limping up to Rufus earlier. It sat in his lap. Rufus calmly held the injured leg with his hand for less than a minute. When the raccoon left and headed back to the wooded area, he no longer limped."

Tamika looks at Carl. "That is amazing! Nothing in the medical industry can justify or testify for such a recovery. How can a robot do that?"

"We have no idea. Judy and I find Rufus acting and performing such amazing feats almost on a daily basis around here."

"Look! That hawk could just reach out and capture the small squirrel. It could have an easy dinner. Yet, none of the prey are concerned. How does Rufus control these animals?" Asks Tamika.

"Our veterinarian tells us that he believes Rufus may emit some kind of high-pitched oral signal that can only be heard by animals. The signal must calm nearby animals to the point they are no longer uneasy among their foes as they are attracted to him."

After several minutes, Carl tells Rufus. "Rufus, why don't you allow the animals to return to their normal daily activity now?" Rufus makes eye contact with each animal and they begin to respond to some signal variance by Rufus and they calmly begin their normal pace back to their area in the woods nearby. They observe as the deer stops and turns her head back to Rufus, as if to thank him.

Again, more tears flowing down Tamika's cheeks.

Billy says. "This is going to be national news worthy. I'm comfortable that no other viewer across the nation has ever seen anything like this."

One by one, everybody returns to the front area of the house.

Billy turns to Carl and Judy. "We thank you for inviting us to your home and sharing Rufus with us."

He then addresses Rufus. "Rufus, we are so impressed with your intelligence and ability to do things beyond our imagination. I can see why Carl and Judy maintain so much respect for you and are happy to have you as part of their family. We thank you for this session and would like to invite your visit to our television station."

"I believe we have completed this segment of our interview. Carl, Judy, I believe a live interview with Rufus would be good for our sister station, FM radio 100.03."

"Will you consider allowing Rufus to participate? A session during Henry's early morning show would be great. Listeners can call in to Rufus with their questions and comments. If Thursday morning will work for you, I'll arrange it."

Rufus nods with his approval.

"Sure." Responds Judy.

"I believe it will provide the community with insight to Rufus's abilities and intelligence." Says Carl.

"Great! I'll have Archie Yokum, our morning show host call you to confirm the talk.

Carl responds. "Rufus and I can do that. What time?"

"Nine o'clock a.m. I recommend Rufus be there at least 10 minutes prior."

"Okay. Rufus, Judy, and I will be at the station well in advance of the show."

Judy speaks up. "I have an early breakfast scheduled with the cards group of ladies on Thursday. Carl you and Rufus can go to the station."

Billy says. "We can tape the show for you to listen in on later."

"Well, thank you. That will be great."

"Okay, we'll see you at the station." Responds Billy.

Outside the house, Flo and assistant pack up the camera equipment and load it back into the van. They pull down the driveway and onto the road toward Country Tour road. Tamika's assistant is driving. Tamika is in the passenger seat and Billy is seated in the rear. Tamika turns to Billy. "I'm still amazed with what I've experienced here. It's almost overwhelming,"

"I know. I don't know what we've got ourselves into. Think about it. We need to protect that family from a yard full of harassing media from all across the nation. But, how? Once we televise this meeting, they will be bombarded with other stations and newspapers at their property.

As Carl and Judy walk through the house, Judy stops. "Carl! When is the breakfast meeting that Rufus will speak at?"

"Oh, that's at seven o'clock tomorrow morning and its' to a group of area business owners and managers."

"Rufus, you're quickly becoming a celebrity in our small town."

Rufus does not comment.

Next day, Carl and Rufus arrive at the seven o'clock Chamber meeting of local businesses fifteen minutes early. They make their way to the meeting room and are promptly greeted by the president of their Chamber of Commerce. "Good morning. You must be Rufus. My name is Sandra Bulzer. I have heard so much about you as I looked forward to this event and meeting you."

"Rufus likes you."

"And you must be Carl Forcrast."

"Yes."

"Carl, you are welcome to sit wherever you prefer. Rufus, why don't you be seated to the right of the podium and then walk to the speaker's podium as I introduce you. Is that okay with you?"

"It is good."

Rufus is the guest speaker that will speak to the group of about forty business managers and owners.

Sandra walks to the podium. "Good morning, everybody. This appears to be the largest attendance we have ever had for chamber meetings. Looking around the room, there is standing room only."

I know everybody is anxious so, it is my pleasure to introduce our speaker. His name is Rufus and he has become a true celebrity in our area. Rufus is a robot. I know you've already heard about this guest, please clap your hands for Rufus!"

As the members and guests clap hands, Rufus peers over the group for several seconds. Then he opens his discussion. "I am honored to stand before you this morning, truly honored. And, as you may know, I have no human emotions, yet I am honored to be here today."

"There are several topics that I could present my view points on today, medical, legal and, world events may be just a few but, I have decided to discuss the national and world political system."

"For your convenience I have electronically accessed all cell phones and turned them to vibrate only. You will still know of calls and messages addressing your phone and be able to respond to any important texts or calls. Your electronics will not interfere with our meeting."

"Are there any elected city or county office holders in attendance today?"

One gentleman raises his hand.

"What is your name sir, and what office do you hold?"

"Elwin Horzon and I am the county tax collector."

"Mr. Horzon. After our discussion, any political ambitions you may have beyond local may be crushed."

Elwin raises his eyebrows and smiles, as he shuffles in his seat.

"Mr. Horzon. I have a quick question of you. Did you receive any bids, any at all?"

"Huh? I'm sorry. Bids?"

"Yes. You returned from your dentist with a new set of teeth. You placed your old false teeth for sale on ebay. Have you had any bids?"

The room broke out in laughter as Rufus followed up with, "That is a joke. I was poking fun at Mr. Horzon. I hope I did not embarrass you sir."

Now, "You go to the poles and cast your vote at election time. In many cases, you may be voting for a person that has never held national position before. Once elected, that freshman congress or senate seat holder arrives in Washington, D.C. and sets up their new office. Soon, a seasoned politician comes to visit and congratulates the freshman for winning the seat. The conversation soon inquires as to what the freshman wants to do for his voters back home. That elected freshman shares his promises back home. The seasoned politician then assures the freshman, "We'll help you get those things introduced in a bill and then, passed". And, we're going to have important bills we will introduce so, we'll need your full support to pass bills that help us politically."

If the newly elected freshman agrees to go along with it, he just became part of the D. C. system. If that newly elected freshman does not go along with the group, he is, so to speak, placed in a political corner and will never get any bill properly introduced or voted on. That newly elected politician may become a short-termed candidate. Their voters back home see him or her as ineffective and probably unworthy of re-election."

"Now, there is another group, lobbyists or insiders that are focused on influencing and directing your candidates voting decisions. Lobbyists do not represent the "back home" voter. They likely are paid millions and even tens of millions of dollars to sway politicians for their introduction of, and pass bills that favor special interests."

Then you have the outsider lobbying. Their objective is to lead the politician astray, into a compromising situation can become an embarrassment, even political suicide if it became publicly known, so the politician just became a puppet for the lobbying agent."

"However, the Lobbying industry is not the only problem. People are being swayed by I. G. P.'s, "Individual and Group Persuaders". Recognized persons may decide they want to change the culture just to prove to themselves they can do it."

"For over two centuries America has been held in place by God. In the seventeenth century God led a group of about fifty men and fourteen women stepped onto this continent, influenced by God for the sole purpose of global expansion in

Christianity. God inspired selected leaders to establish and draft the Constitution. America became the most respected nation, a true world leader in Christianity, military power, industry, and financials, all toward the greatness for humanity worldwide.

"Now I'll firmly say this! (pause) There is a Greater Being. You call Him "God." You need to pay attention! I can prove that God exists. You see, I have more "smarts" up here than you do. I have access to information that you don't even know exists. So, I hope accept and understand Rufus when Rufus says, "There is a Greater Being, God.""

"There is a bad guy in the mix. He was once an angel and part of God's world. Satan was cast out of heaven along with his personal angels. In denial of God, Satan began concentrating on your planet, earth. Satan's goal, (and he believes he can) is to overtake God, is to direct people away from God's Son, Jesus Christ. Jesus is the only way for humans to be with God someday."

"There is a particular movement in the advanced stages that has programmed people to communicate by texting and non-verbal means of communication. Why is that important to Satan? People are no longer interacting with each other emotionally, verbally. Society no longer desires to have conversation with each other and, they are more comfortable sending and receiving messages electronically. Population is easier to control when they are not "talking" about issues."

"And, average people today dress casually, in some cases, too casually to the point of not feeling worthy of wearing a coat or suit. At a point, the only people wearing suits will be your leaders, leaders that are becoming more and more under the direct influence of Satan. You are looked upon as the little people, and will always look up to the best dressed with a sense of greater respect and admiration, even though the respect may not be deserved."

Rufus turns to Carl. "Carl, will you come up and share your story on dress code?"

'Yes."

"I will share this as an example. A friend of mine, I'll refer to as Tom. Tom entered the Post Office lobby and stood in line with about eleven others. After conducting his postal business, he left. He smiled to himself because more than half the people at the post office smiled and spoke, as they acknowledged Tom."

"A few days later, Tom returned to the post office. He was again in a long line as he waited his turn. He was dressed in jeans and sport shirt. Upon returning to his car, it stood out to Tom that not one person responded to his "good morning" or, even his eye contact and a nod."

"Now, why is that?" Tom thought.

"So, Tom tried it again. He drove the same vehicle and wore the same style clothes as the first visit. When Tom left the lobby, dressed in his suit and tie, strangers acknowledged his presence."

"Who dresses for pride and self esteem? Who commands respect? And, how do they command respect? Politicians. Politicians in elected offices, state and national. They dress in tailor made suits when in public view and it works well for them. Why is it important to them to keep the general population dressed down?"

"Lowering the self esteem of the general population makes citizens easier to manage. Easily managed people become "little people" that are insignificant in the eyes of the self-proclaimed elite."

Security approaches the microphone as Rufus steps back. "Rufus is in high demand these days. Ladies and gentlemen, Rufus has another meeting scheduled in town and must leave."

Rufus then steps up. "It's unfortunate that we have so little time because there is much up for discussion. I will leave you with this, there is a solution that brings leaders back in line, that deals with rioting, murders, and theft, just to mention a few. In other words, at a later meeting, I will disclose to you exactly what I know that you and others can do about all the doom and gloom out there. So, in the meantime, look forward to a peaceful existence here in America.

Rufus waves to the audience. "Thank you. I hope you all have a great day", as he and Carl are escorted from the room by security.

Sandra steps up to the microphone. "Wasn't Rufus spectacular?" Showing their appreciation to Rufus, the entire room stands and claps hands."

"We will now ask Joe Chipmon to come up and update us on the Chamber's upcoming annual meeting."

Outside, as Carl unlocks the car, "Rufus, I must say that I am even more amazed with your ability to openly discuss matters that are far beyond human comprehension and knowledge. But you explain each topic in a way that is easily understood by the listener."

Carl hurriedly drives away from the building and turns left on Mason Drive toward the television station for their appointment. The drive is less than five minutes. He pulls his car to the entrance. At this time of the morning, most parking spots are available as he selects one. They are greeted at the door by Tamika. "Right on time. That's great. Follow me and I'll introduce you to our engineer."

Walking down the short hall and turning right into the news room where the engineer quickly attaches hands free mic and ear phones on Rufus. He turns to Carl. "Do you want to participate in the interview, sir?"

"No. Rufus will handle it well."

"Okay. We'll seat you near Rufus for the upcoming session."

A door opens as another person enters the studio. "Good morning. I'm Stewart Call. You must be Mr. Forcrast. And you're Rufus! It's such a pleasure to finally meet you both."

Carl recognizes Stewart from his six o'clock am daily television show.

Stewart explains, "You may know that we have blocked out the normal morning show and replaced it today with this special broadcast. We've advertised over the last forty-eight hours and expect a great participation."

Stewart turns toward an assistant. "Help me get these electronics hooked up around my body and we'll start the live show in exactly forty-one seconds."

"Rufus, we'll be inviting people to call in with their questions and comments. Are you ready?"

"Rufus is ready."

Stewart is quiet as he hears the engineer. "Ten, nine, eight, seven, six, five, four, three, two, one."

"Good morning, and welcome to the Stewart's call-in show. Today is a special day and we have a very special guest with us. Let me introduce Carl Forcrast on my left and on my right is none other than Rufus, our own hometown celebrity intelligent robot."

Rufus looks to the camera and nods his head then, turns back facing Stewart.

"It looks like we're going to have a special day. All the lines are lit up with incoming calls. If you do call and get a busy signal, just continue to call back. And, you may be on hold for an extended period of time."

"Our first call is from Mackie. Go ahead Mackie."

"Rough House, What do you do in spare time? Observe people with your silly ways? What do you eat? Caster Oil? You think you're a preacher? You say there is a God? Really? Where is that God? Why doesn't He do something to help people rather than kill them?"

"Thank you, "Tackie". I prefer encouraging others to study the bible. What would I learn from a preaching human? And, I'm not familiar with the Caster oil. How does it taste?"

"I'm certain that you've been programmed with ultra-conservative, left wing views, right?"

"Rufus's intelligence is expanded by worldwide history, current worldly events, medical, political, and legalities, all of which is updated on an ongoing basis."

"Ok. You're so smart? How many years did president Charles Hall serve as president of the United States?

"Charles Hall served from December, 1863 until December, 1914. Charles Martin Hall never served as president of The United States. Charles M. Hall was founder and president of Alcoa Aluminum Corporation.

"Okay Rough house! Very quickly now, what is the simple mathematics of two thousand six hundred three point nine times four hundred thirty-one point three and then divided by eleven hundred seventy-one point five?"

Immediately, Rufus answers. "Nine hundred fifty-eight point sixty-five".

"Mackie. I like you. I can detect that you possess a sharp mind. Now, would you like to participate in a similar, but much simpler equation?"

"Go for it!"

Within ten seconds, what is four times five plus seven hundred eighty-five, divided by two?"

"Why would I even attempt to solve that mathematical equation. That's silly of you to even ask anybody to attempt."

Stewart speaks up. "Okay. Ten seconds has lapsed. Let's take another call. On line four is Katherine."

"Katherine, what is your question of Rufus?"

"What makes you think there is a God?"

"What makes you think there is no God? If you do not believe in God, then you believe in Satan and are carrying out Satan's will. It's as simple as that. Do you accept the fact that God does have power to control, even plants and animals? In the house where I reside with Carl and Judy, there is a Christmas cactus. That cactus blooms once a year, during the Christmas season, a time when Christians celebrate the birth of God's son, Jesus Christ. Do you believe that is a coincidence?"

"How or why would a God do that?"

"God shows humans that he does have the power to perform such enjoyable features on earth for mankind to enjoy. Believe that."

"I prefer a more convincing answer. If that's your best answer I'll end my call now."

Line four lost the call from Katherine.

"On line two is Roy. Go ahead Roy."

"Rufus, my name is Roy."

"Thank you for joining us this morning, Roy".

"I love the Lord and have been involved in my church for more than ten years. Sometimes, when I share my faith with others, I encounter questions that I cannot answer in a way that makes sense to the non-believer. I approached my pastor recently and asked him to meet with me so I could share the few questions that I stumble on as I attempt answering them with street level terms that will make sense to the person.

My pastor mumbled, "So, you want a Q & A session. He then walked away. I determined that to be disrespectful to the Lord and now I'm considering leaving that church. What is your advice?"

"When you attending this church, during worship, do you sense the presence of the spirit?"

"Well, sometimes I do."

"Then remain in your present church. Pastors are human and they have emotions. Your pastor may have an underlying conflict that discouraged a meeting. The spirit of the Lord is most important to you so you should certainly remain at that church. Some other churches hold Sunday services and the Spirit is not present. The Spirit bearing down in your church is fulfilling. Find another person, such as a deacon or elder for your answers. You are very fortunate to experience the Lord's Spirit while in church. You may feel goose bumps when the song or message is about God. You are fortunate."

"Another caller, Rufus."

"Hi Rufus. Rufus, my name is Wilma."

"What is your personal opinion of how God created the universe? And, I read that our planet is millions of years old. Yet, the bible says only a few thousand years."

"God knows. Rufus has no opinion. Rufus is a robot. Rufus only considers facts. Your bible dates back a few thousand years and that may not be the origin of the planet."

"I have a question for you, Wilma. Do you believe that dinosaurs existed millions of years ago on your planet?"

"No. I do not."

"Why not?"

"Because earth has not been here for millions of years. And, scientific aging is based on the age of carbon associated with the bones and those readings are false, in error."

"Okay. Here's your what if? As an example of time that is quoted in your bible, God tells you that a day in heaven may be like a thousand years on earth. So, he built everything from heaven in six days. On the seventh day, He rested. What if each day in heaven may be several thousand or, millions of years?"

"Okay. Consider this. Along the days in heaven compared to many years on earth, dinosaurs and neanderthals date back thirty-five million years as they roamed earth. All such creatures died at relatively the very same time and it is assumed by scientists that a meteor impacted the planet. Dust, in an unimaginable volume became airborne and keeping the sun light and heat from reaching earth. Most living species died. God had a reason for the demise of life on earth. He then caused everything humans enjoy viewing today, fresh plants to grow, animals to live, and finally mankind in His own image, still everything within heavens six days of creation. On the seventh day, He rested."

Another Caller. "My name is Harvey and my question is, are we in danger of a nuclear attack?"

"There is a danger"

"When?"

"I am not able to reveal the future. Only God can do that."

"Alright, Rufus. Who will be the next president of the United States?"

"The person with the most votes. I am unable to accurately predict the individual.

"Okay smartie. You talk about global love. How can we have global love?"

"First, recognize the prevention of love. Satan is in the heart of haters and sinners. Satan and his followers of about one third of the angels in heaven were cast out by God. Satan thrives on your sins and hatred because, in his mind, you are turning to him instead of God. He corrupts your society with hatred. You can see the hatred in persons demonstrating in the streets. Now, if those demonstrators developed a deep love for all other humans, how much hatred would there be?"

"Look at the total of souls since America was first occupied by Christians.

"The Mayflower had 19 women on board and three were pregnant. At the 1620-21 feast, fourteen women participated. The life span in 1700's and 1800's ranged between the ages of thirty-six and forty-one. There have been more than 27 family generations between 1620 and 1970. Those generations have produced an estimated 849 million men and women in the United States, of which 773 million have accepted Christianity and the majority of the remaining 76 million basically have no beliefs. Satan can never influence a majority of people away from God.

"My point is that Satan wants to turn Christians from God and it can never happen.

"Some would like to think Christianity is fading and Satan is winning. Wrong. God has already won! If he came today, since America was founded God would be responsible for over 773 million Christians. And that does not include all the American missionaries across the planet that continually expose, persuade, and develop Christians in other countries. Satan has failed his spiteful mission to turn most Christians against God."

"Wow! Thank you, Rufus. You have given me something to think about."

"Thank you, Harvey, for sharing your time with us."

Another caller. "My name is Roger. Tell me why I should accept all the stuff that there is a God. I believe we evolved over millions of years."

"Rufus will share some data and information, directly from God's creations."

1. Our planet recycles life-friendly carbon. Carbon dioxide traps heat and keeps the planet warm enough to support life, specifically created human life.

2. We have an ozone layer that blocks harmful rays

   "Ancient plantlike organisms in the oceans added oxygen to the atmosphere and created a high-altitude layer of ozone that shielded early land species from lethal radiation.", Specifically created for human life.

3. The moon stabilizes our axial wobble, specifically created for human life.

4. Our varied surfaces support many life forms, specifically created for human life.

5. We have a magnetic field that deflects solar outbursts and radiation, specifically created for human life.

6. We're situated at just the exact distance from the sun that allows water and life, specifically created for human life.

7. We're situated safely away from giant gases If other planets were closer, their gravity pull could cause disaster for earth, specifically created for human life.

8. Earth's sun is stable as a huge star. A smaller sun (star) would be short lived and would give off bursts of harmful radiation.

9. Our dynamic core contains radioactive elements that protects the planet from solar flares, specifically created for human life.

10. Giant planets thin out the asteroid belt, protecting earth from frequent collisions, specifically created for human life.

11. The sun protects earth from galactic debris from interstellar space, specifically created for human life.

12. Earth's galactic path steers it clear of hazards as the solar system is in a safe harbor between spiral arms, in

its circular orbit avoids the galaxy's inner regions, specifically created for human life.

13. Earth's stellar location reduces gravitational tugs, gamma ray busts, or collapsing stars called supernovae, specifically created for human life.

Roger responds, "Impressive. Beyond my understanding but, I guess its impressive."

"Thank you, Roger. That data was a lot to absorb. If you would like a copy, you may contact me through this station. Have a great day."

Stewart peers at the time and announces, "We have time for one more call. On the line is Jerry."

"Jerry, welcome to the show."

"Thanks. I have a question for Rufus. Personally, I believe Rufus is an idiot, he has no common sense! I want to hear his response to socialism. I am a devout socialist. So, go for it Rufus."

"Good morning Jerry. My direct response to your cause is easily addressed. Let me invite you to step back and use your imagination to look down on this planet and view each country, how it fits into the world scene."

"The United States of America has been the envy of most every other country on the planet since the constitution was signed. Over the years, your country has been the financial foundation for the world. Americans have been the milestone for others. The Christian faith was an envy worldwide. Countries used communism as they attempted to compete with the personal opportunities and growth of America. Overall, Americans have been far happier, wealthier, and more fundamentally sound than in any other country. The awesome military forces protected America and other countries during conflicts. America and Americans as a whole have been admired by all. That admiration created competition, anxiety, and hatred by some governments and dictatorships. No other country could defeat America with military force."

"Stay with me now, Jerry. This is important."

"Their socialist economies were trying and substandard, and insufficient to Capitalism in America. So, Russia declared they would take over your United States of America from within. By the late 1950's the education system began being infiltrated by communism. Their goal was to expand the teachings of students toward the benefits of communism over capitalism. They were very talented and scientific in "brainwashing" America's young people. Over several decades, those young brainwashed students have grown to be university professors, politicians, and persons of influence over others. Studies about American history, murdering of jews, along with all other books that contradicted their goals were eliminated. What you see now is the elevation of communism to socialism. So, what exactly is socialism? The socialistic agenda today is another step toward communism. Socialists can own property, until it is taken away and extended to communism."

"Socialism promotes happiness when life's essentials are free to all when they share in everything, the economy, lifestyle, food, and enjoyment of a great life. That is until the majority of America's population submits to all the free stuff."

"Then, freebies decline. The governing few will take over your assets, your property, and move you from a nice two thousand square foot home to a small six hundred feet high-rise apartment. Loyal people to the dictatorship will take over your property and live comfortably as long as they remain loyal. You will be rationed for food, public transportation provided to and from restricted areas. The American of today is then reduced to a total dependency on a dictatorial governing body. Now, and only then, will jealous countries see you as no longer a threat to them. All will be equal. Except, the American military that has protected the United States and other countries will be subordinate to communism and socialism with America's sale of most all its guns, planes, ships, etc. to China."

"China now owns more than 146,000 acres of America's farm land. Does that make you happy?"

"Rufus, you don't have a clue. Everything you say is warped. False."

"Do you have a grandparent that is living today?"

"Have you had a conversation with your elder family about capitalism verses socialism?"

"No way. They are too opinionated. They won't listen to why socialism is best for everybody."

"Rufus, you're a piece of plastic, metal, outdated computer driven. I thought you were supposed to be intelligent! That's absurd. You are trying to scare everybody. Socialism is a movement in this country and your stupid words make no sense. You'll be the first to be eliminated, and in due time. Good bye!"

Stewart speaks. "Today has been a terrific show. Rufus, do you have a final message for our audience?"

"I do. People hold individuals accountable for their political issues. That should not be the case."

"Congressman Bublyorkze is actively pursuing a bill that totally changes the constitution of your United States. You may hold Bublyorkze with some degree of hatred for his beliefs. After all, Bublyorkze believes he is doing the right thing. He is not the problem."

"In 1930 in Robinsonville, Mississippi, 19-year-old Robert Johnson is claimed to have sold his soul to the devil at the intersection of highways 61 and 48. Robert had inspirations to play a guitar. He could not even strum a note. He vanished for a year. Nobody knew where he was. When he reappeared, his guitar music was exceptional, enough to record twenty-nine songs until his death at age 27. Before becoming famous, he is documented as praying to Satan and basically exchanging his soul for a life of success. On his death bed, he attempted to negotiate with Satan for the release of that bind. Satan would not release his bond, and Christ would not hear his crying prayers."

"Other successful people that allegedly exchanged their soul for success include inventor Jack Parsons, entertainer Bob Dylan, guitarist Jimmy Page, composer Philippe Musard, and Catholic Priest Father Urbain Grandier.

"Back to Cubborkze, at some point in his life, he exchanged his soul for all the money and power his now possesses. He does not realize his bond to Satan and may not even recall declaring a worship for Satan. If in your heart, you know right from wrong, you are able to identify Satan's "soldiers" that act in ways that are not God's intent. Your bible tells you that Satan has been turned loose here on earth to turn as many of God's people against Him as he can. That is real. You may not like the past ruler of Soviet Union. That ruler did not acknowledge God and sold out their soul to Satan. Fact!"

"Okay, that was the last call on today's show. Rufus and Carl, I thank you for sharing your time with us this morning. We'd like to invite you back again in the near future. Think we can plan that?"

Carl responds. "Absolutely. Don't you agree, Rufus?"

"Rufus agrees."

As Carl and Rufus leave the station. "Why are you so quiet, Rufus?

"An important event is taking place is in the local news, live right now."

"What is it?" As Carl turns up the volume on his car radio.

"This is breaking news. Two men have barricaded themselves with hostages inside the Markentile Credit Union on Eagle Nest road. It is believed the suspects are the same two that escaped from the county jail earlier this morning. We have received word that one of their hostages is twelve-year old Barbie Mergerint, the step-daughter of professional quarterback Frank Mergerint. Barbie's mother, Lucy Mergerint passed away after a short illness. Our news team is on the way to the site and we'll keep you updated as news develops. Stay tuned to this station.

Rufus asks. "You know the Mergerint family, don't you?"

"Frank Mergerint's step-daughter?"

CHAPTER 9

Carl applies the car's brakes and promptly pulls to the side of the street. In his alarmed state of mind, he attempts to understand what he just heard.

"My brother, Cramer's first wife was pregnant when they divorced? Our family did not know that! Lucy never told Cramer about her pregnancy or, about a daughter? And here I am hearing about all this on the radio?"

Sitting quietly, Carl stares out across a nearby park, as he attempts to gather his thoughts. "I have a niece? How do I tell Cramer? He has no ideal that his wife was expecting at the time they split and divorced? This is awful!"

He reaches for his phone and dials Cramer's cellular number. After several rings, the message tells him to leave a message. "Cramer, this is Carl. Call me as soon as you hear this message. I love you, brother."

"I've got to do something! That child is my niece! And nobody in the family is there for her."

Carl continues mumbling as he puts his car in drive and continues down the street, trying to learn where that warehouse is located. He calls back to the television station. The lines are all busy. Dialing the local police department. "What is the location of that credit union where the little girl is hostage?"

"Sir, the public is forbidden to go near the crime location. You're better off to stay tuned to local news for updates."

"But…." The connection is lost.

Rufus provides instructions, "Carl, turn right 2 miles ahead onto Railroad street. The credit union is at the corner of Railroad and Bunker Avenue."

"Thank you, Rufus."

As they speed toward the destination, Rufus warns Carl. "You are not driving safely. You must concentrate on arriving safely."

"And, you're right. I'll slow down."

Carl attempts to approach the area but, police are diverting all traffic away from the crime vicinity. He nears the officer and rolls down his window.

"Officer, my niece is the hostage. I need to get to the scene."

"Sir, the public is forbidden to go beyond this point. You need to follow other traffic away from this area."

"But I may be able to help."

"Sir! You must turn left and proceed down that street."

Carl obeys and calmly follows other traffic away from the crime area. Frustrated, he wants to be helpful but, in reality, he realizes he can be of little to no assistance. He realizes that Barbie doesn't know him, even though they are so closely related.

"Cramer is apparently busy and has no idea that a hostage situation holds his daughter captive. He's probably in a meeting or is out of cellular range and not available."

Rufus speaks up. "Carl, turn right and into the alley ahead. You will be able to drive within two blocks of the credit union."

"Thank you! Thank you! Thank you!" Says Carl as he slows down to make the turn.

He eases down the narrow alley for a block as it narrows to a police barricade. He looks around for a place to park his car and recognizes his best option is at the rear door of a retail store building. He and Rufus exit the vehicle and make their way closer to the crime area where a taped off area prevents them from going further. Carl leans over the tape as he looks around. There are up to twenty other spectators observing the standoff. Two visible snipers on nearby roofs and in position for orders to react.

A police sergeant holding a speaker turns toward the spectators. "please remain outside the taped perimeter!"

Carl obeys and walks toward his car. "I guess there is nothing
I can do here." He tells Rufus.

"About all I can do at this point is to continue calling Cramer.
He needs to be here.

For Cramer to hear the news about Barbie from me rather
than the radio station is so important."

Carl asks Rufus, "Do you know of anything we can do?"

He turns to look at Rufus. "Rufus? Rufus! Rufus! Oh no!
Now, where is that boy?"

"No response. Now Carl is upset. He wants to leave the area
but, Rufus is nowhere to be seen. He turns around and runs back
to the taped off scene screaming. "Rufus! Rufus! Still no response.

Two nearby police hastily approach Carl. "Sir, please step
back and remain outside that line."

"Who are you calling out for?"

"My friend. He is in this area and I can't find him. It's okay.
Thanks."

Carl walks back toward his car while looking back and all
around for any sign of Rufus. "Where in the heck is that jerk? I
can't leave without him!"

He can't continue to block the back doorway of the retail store
and has no choice but to back his car out of the alley and vacate
the area. He thinks. "I cannot go off and leave Rufus wondering
around here. Whatever he is up to, it is no good."

He considers. "I'll park over on Walker Drive and walk back
as close as allowed. Hopefully, I'll spot Rufus and get him away
from here."

A portable modular unit has been set up as a police command
center. Sirens are approaching as two unmarked police vehicles
escort a SUV to the central the command center. Carl watches
to see who or what this vehicle is delivering. All three vehicles
come to a halt and the SUV right rear door swings open. Out
steps Frank Mergerint. Police quickly escort him into the command center.

Carl thinks. "It's probably not normal for a close relative to become directly involved in any such hostage situation. With Frank's step-daughter in the custody of the kidnappers, maybe the negotiators can use Mergerint toward a solution."

Carl continues to watch for Rufus. "That rascal is up to no good! I can sense it."

His cell phone rings. He recognizes the number as Judy's. "Hello."

"Carl, have you heard the news? Frank Mergerint's daughter has been kidnapped."

"I know. I am at the scene now. Rufus was with me, and now I can't find him. He just vanished!"

"Oh no. What are you going to do?"

"Don't be concerned. I'll locate him."

"Okay. Be careful and keep me informed."

Police have been attempting normal communication strategies with the robbers inside the credit union. No response so far. Police have heard unusual sounds coming from inside the building. It lasted about ten minutes and stopped.

Police sergeant Welch turned to sergeant Mack. "Did that sound to you as an attempt to break in to the credit union safe?"

"Hmmm, it could be. But, doubtful."

"Rufus! Rufus!" Carl screams out as he spots Rufus walking at a distance, through the police barricade toward the rear of a nearby warehouse. No response from Rufus.

Rufus ignores a policeman's command and approaches the rear of the building.

The credit union building is surrounded by armed police as Rufus still makes his way toward the rear.

"Captain Ramsey! Billings here. I'm near the back door and this robot-like thing is nearing the rear door"

"Okay everybody, hold your position and await orders."

Things seem to be in slow motion during these tense moments. Adrenalin is peaked. Corporal Billing's eyes focused on Rufus as they await orders.

Sergeant Creel eases up toward Billings and whispers, "That robot is opening the back door. The door is locked but he is opening it."

"How? That door requires a key along with electronic codes in the panel. He can't open that door."

"I know. But he has now eased the door open. Should we rush him?"

"Captain Ramsey says for everybody to hold positions."

Creel thinks. "Nothing like this has ever been experienced. It's not in the training manual. Nobody seems to have a quick answer."

Rufus is now inside and quietly eased the door closed.

Creel now notifies Captain Ramsey, "Sir, that robot has now entered the building through the locked rear door. It's inside!"

"Are you sure? How did it get inside? The hostage takers had to let it in and it's part of their plan. Remain steady and let's continue to follow procedural protocol"

Rufus is inside and police are unable to determine what is happening inside the building.

Captain Ramsey turns to lieutenant Neal. "That dadgum robot is involved! That's how it entered the building."

"Corporal Binkston, continue calling the credit union phone. See if you can get an answer."

Binkston allows the phone to ring eleven times. No response.

"Keep dialing that number. Continue trying."

In the meantime, Captain Ramsey orders the snake. A snake is an electronic spy piece that can slither beneath the door and relay back to the screen all activity from inside the building. Sergeant. Camden is in charge of the procedure.

Camden goes to the front corner of the building, then sneaks beneath the windows to the front door. In position, he begins positioning the snake.

Inside, somebody answers the phone.

"H-Hello."

Suddenly, Captain Ramsey rushes to Neal's side.

"This is officer Neal with the police department. Who am I talking to?"

"I'm Anna Lewis, the assistant manager."

In a calming voice, "Anna, is everybody okay?"

"We're all okay. Just scared. That's all."

"Thanks for answering the telephone so we can work toward getting you out of there."

"Yes sir. They disconnected the office phone and I plugged it in again."

"Anna, how many intruders are there?"

"Two."

"May I speak with one of the hostage takers?"

"They are not here. They left. We were instructed to stay in this building for thirty minutes or be killed."

"Anna. Where have they gone?"

"I don't know. They went to another room and may have gone out the back door."

"Anna. We have officers posted around the building and they did not leave your building. They are still inside."

"We must have access to the inside. I need you to unlock the front door."

Silence.

"Anna? Anna? Are you there, Anna?"

"Officer, this is Rufus. Rufus is a robot. Anna fainted. She is going to be okay."

Officer Neal covers the phone and whispers to Captain Ramsey. "This is that stupid robot!"

Ramsey takes the phone. "This is Captain Ramsey of the police department. You are a robot?"

"Yes, I am. I am Rufus."

"I've heard about you from our local news. Where are your partners?"

"I have no partners."

"Mr. Rufus, we know that you are involved in this hostage and robbery. I need you and your two accomplices to surrender and, one-by-one exit the front door. Nobody will harm you if you do as I say. Do you understand me?"

"Rufus is here to help. Rufus is not involved in any crime. Rufus will exit the building after the employees and customers exit."

Captain Ramsey alerts all officers of what they may expect.

Rufus opens the front door. "Barbie, you may go first."

"Anna, please help the older gentleman and you both leave now."

Rufus tells hostages, "You may leave the building. Tell police the building is now secured by Rufus."

Outside, the officers brisk the hostages away to the command center asking each, "Do you know where the men are that attempted to, or did rob the bank?"

"They are no longer in the building." is the typical answer"

Captain Ramsey alerts his department, "They are still hiding in the building. There are three, not two. Bucky, you and your men secure the building and negotiate those thugs out."

"Yes sir."

"Open the front door. Do it now! You have no means of escape. Come out one-by-one and nobody gets hurt. Open the door and walk out!"

Captain Ramsey gathers his team. "Now things are clearing up a little. The two men inside worked with that robot, letting him inside and now all three are inside. Cooper, go to the bank door and test it for opening. I doubt that it will be open but, let's take that as a first step."

"Lt. Bishop, have your negotiating skills sharpened. We need to negotiate the safety of those hostages and reach a surrender of the hostage holders. Negotiating will be our remaining plan. Got it?"

"Yes sir."

Officer Cooper approaches the front door of the building, reaching for the handle when the door suddenly opens. Shocked, he steps back two steps and points his firearm directly at Rufus's head and begins screaming. Get on the floor! Do it now! Get to the floor!"

Rufus remains steadfast. Four policemen ease through the door and into the lobby, all with pistols drawn.

Two of the police have guns pointed directly at Rufus.

Rufus speaks. "I am here to help you. Ease your weapons. I will work with you to solve the situation."

Screams coming from multiple police officers are telling Rufus, "Get on the floor! Do it! Do it now!"

Still astonished with a lack of response to their orders, the officers remain in position with guns focused on Rufus.

Police are still convinced this robot is part of the hostage situation. Captain Ramsey orders his team to quickly escort the hostages away from the building and directly to the temporary headquarters for their safety. Sergeant Mitchell and Parks are told to escort Rufus to a nearby building for interrogation, in hopes they can actually interrogate a robot. If not, their specialty team will be brought in to attempt electronically retrieve information from Rufus. Sergeant Parks attempts but, Rufus refuses to accept being handcuffed.

"I will go with you. I will go of my own free will. You may not bind my hands", says Rufus.

They finally agree and escort Rufus to a nearby building to initiate their interrogation.

Ramsey orders remaining officers to search the entire credit union building for those two other robbers. He is still convinced that Rufus is a main player in the robbery.

"That robot has the answers we need."

After five short minutes, the searching officers return to the to the credit union lobby.

"Captain, we have found nobody in our search. We're amazed. This is weird. Nobody else in this building."

"Amazed? You're amazed? I'm amazed that we are accepting it that two men and an undetermined amount of cash has just disappeared in thin air. Continue searching. They are hiding somewhere in this building."

In the meantime, Sergeant Mitchell and Parks begin their interrogation and are pulling no information from Rufus. He is willing to work with them in an effort to solve the robbery but, they remain convinced that he is really the brains behind the heist. So, they're to a point of calling in the electronics team to retrieve the necessary information.

At the bank, one of the officers called out, "Captain Ramsey, you need to see this!"

"Okay."

"We moved this large cabinet away from the wall and look what we discovered! The large hole in this wall appears to go outside and then inside something dark."

"You've got to be kidding me!"

Jentzen quickly reacts and decides to walk outside and look at this wall area!

"I want to know what we're dealing with here."

He exits the rear door and runs around the corner to see only a blank wall with no visible hole. Puzzled, he thinks, "We saw a hole in the inside wall that should be visible on the outside but, there is no outside hole. The only thing visible along this wall is an air conditioning unit."

He steps over to look behind the air conditioning unit. As he leans on the air unit, he notices the AC housing box is unstable. It moves easily. He slides the hull away from the wall. "Aha! This is only the outer shell for an air conditioner. It was placed here as a cover and distraction. Inside this box, there is no air conditioning unit."

"Hey guys! This dips down into a tunnel. The robbers came out through the wall and into this false air conditioning case cover and then dropped down inside their tunnel and crawled along its way. It's all covered on the outside to appear as though an air unit is in place. There is no a/c unit here, only the outer cover."

Captain Ramsey observes the location of the empty box. "Pretty slick, the parking lot is on the west side of the building and the drive through for ATM banking turns onto Pinkley Drive.

This side of the building is seldom noticed by the employees. So, this extra box was never noticed."

He looks around the group. "Russ, all your working out is now important to us. As the smaller of our group, remove your excess attachments, go down inside the tunnel opening and tell me what you see."

"Yes sir."

Russ quickly sheds his firearm belt and other attachments so he can fit in the tunnel more easily. He eases down and into the opening, head first.

"What do you see, Russ?"

"I can't tell for certain. I estimate it to be about seventy-five long. I can see a dim light shining in the end, from above"

"So, the tunnel is straight? Going eastward?"

"Yes sir."

"Okay. Come back out of the tunnel. Go with me and Dwight."

Captain Ramsey leads the two officers out the front door. "Seventy-five feet? In that eastward direction? That goes directly toward that small house, next door to the credit union. Come on, let's check it out."

At the house next door, both the front and rear doors are locked. With the dwelling now surrounded they knock on the door while exerting caution in case people are inside. Finally checking windows, On the far side of the house, next to the concrete driveway, they find one window open. Dwight opens the window and calls out warning. "This is the police. Anybody inside this building must quickly identify yourself, surrender and move to the center room."

No response

Russ then crawls through the window opening and with his firearm drawn, he searches every room and closet, he then signals to the others that all is clear. Dwight then crawls through as Captain Ramsey tells Russ to open the front door. Ramsey approaches the front and signals for sergeant Sewell and Tarpley standing in front of the credit union building to come over, quickly.

Inside the old house and in the large west side room, they view the floor all torn up with a large hole near the outer wall.

Captain Ramsey concludes, "That hole is an entrance to the tunnel and connects this old empty house to the credit union building. Guys, the robbers spent a lot of time in advance as they manually dug out that tunnel in expectations of their robbery. And now we know what caused the pounding noise we heard earlier. They were knocking out part of the wall to then enter the AC unit and the tunnel."

Corporal Tidwell speaks up. "I know the person that owns this house. He's retired and lives near me."

"Get him on the phone! I want to talk with him."

Ramsey, with his cell phone, makes a call. "Hey Mitchell. Any progress with that robot? Is he giving us any information?"

"No sir. Not yet. I have called our electronics team to bring necessary equipment and come quickly. The robot may need to be de-programmed electronically in order to retrieve the information we need."

"Good. That's good. Keep me posted."

"Captain, I've got Corbett Hugolbotham, the owner of this house on the phone."

"Good. Let me talk to him."

"Sir, I am Captain Ramsey with the police department. Assuming you were not directly involved, has this house at 9078 Run Wild Lane been rented or occupied?"

"Yes sir."

"To whom?"

"I'm not sure."

"A man called me back in March in response to my rental ad. It's an old house and doesn't rent for very much. He was calling me while traveling and wanted to rent it for one year. He said he would pay six months in advance and would sign a rental agreement if I would leave it and a key beneath the door mat. The next day I received a money order for the six months rent.

I placed the rental form and key at the front door. I have never met the renter."

"Did they sign the form? Do you have any record of their name, like on the money order?"

"Nope. I didn't receive the rental form back and I guess it didn't concern me too much because of the front money."

"The renter made a large hole in your floor, then dug a long tunnel to the credit union building next door. Let me ask you this. Have you driven by here and noticed any vehicle parked in the driveway or on the property? Noticed anything unusual whatsoever?"

"No sir. I may have driven by a couple of times. But I guess everything appeared normal to me."

"Okay. Thank you, Sir. It is urgent that we contact the renter. If you think of any other information, please call me quickly. I may be in touch with you again on this matter. I appreciate your help. Have a good day."

Russ's phone rings! "Hello!"

"Hi hon. You got a minute? Our daughter is pregnant. Isn't that exciting?"

"Sorry hon. Later!" Click.

Captain Ramsey tells others. "It's apparent the crooks robbed the credit union and, unnoticed by the employees, came to this house underground with the money. Their exit through this window is obvious. With a vehicle probably parked near the window, they calmly drove away."

"Hey, Howard, establish an estimated time they left the area and put your guys contacting businesses that have cameras. Log all vehicle identities that were driving on any street away from this crime scene.

"Okay you guys, let's secure the house from any intruders and return to the bank area. It's time for our investigators to perform their expertise. We'll stay out of their way."

Back with their attempts at pulling information from Rufus, Mitchell and Parks are taking on the good guy, bad guy role at the interrogation. They are very focused on quickly pulling information from Rufus that points to the others involved, and where they are now located, along with the money stolen.

"Mr. Robot, my name is Lin Mitchell, a sergeant in special ops section. I'm here to help you get through this entanglement you are in. This is sergeant Carrel Parks. a special negotiator for the department."

"Robot! you are the ring leader of this robbery! We know that! Your partners are both in our custody now. One is scared, scared enough to spill his guts out and work with our officers in exchange for consideration at his trial. He is telling us everything, including your role. I just got word that, unless you open up and help us solve this robbery, you will soon be secluded and then totally disconnected from your power source, to then become a piece of nothing. You will be unable to see any humans again, ever. And, I just learned that your owner has been apprehended. He faces twenty years in prison, just for his involvement in bringing you to this site for criminal purposes. So, Mr. Robot! It's time for you to fess up. Tell us everything about the robbery, from the planning stages to the robbery and holding of hostages."

"You understand the trouble you're in, don't you? You know the unlawful situation that you have pulled your owner into, don't you? You're only a computer, plastics, metal, and imitation flesh. So, there is no reason for you to withhold information from us, information that is vital to lightening the charges against you and your owner. So, tell me everything! How did you involve the other two men to assist you in this crime?" Silence.

Lt. Parks speaks up. "Robot, would you like something to help you relax? Are you comfortable? Let's you and I talk. How long have you been associated with your owners, Mr. and Mrs. Forcast? Are they a good family?" Silence.

Officer Mitchell blares out! "Look! robot! Knock of the squeeze tactic with us. Either you tell us what we need to know, and do it now, or we pull Mrs. Forcast in for a hard drilling interview. You can save the Forcast family from all the anguish they are about to face. It's tough. In fact, it's horrible. We're trying to help you. You do realize that don't you? You need to open up right now and tell us the complete details of this robbery." Silence.

These police fail to realize they are facing a much higher level of negotiating, knowledge, and extreme abilities that are unavailable to humans. As Mitchell hammers Rufus to open discussions with him, Rufus is Focused on the quieter sergeant Parks. Within less than thirty seconds, with eye-to-eye contact with Parks, Rufus has quieted him down totally. He has hypnotized officer Parks into a trance, and is awaiting further instructions from Rufus.

Rufus then begins to talk softly to officer Mitchell. "Sir, I want to comply with your wishes and."

"Then, do it! Give me answers and do it now! Do you understand me?"

Rufus responds. "Yes sir. I understand what you want and I am prepared to help you and your police department to solve this case. There seems to be something in my left eye. Sir, can you see it? It is bothering me."

"Hmmmm."

Now, in their trance, both officers are awaiting instructions from Rufus. "Officer Mitchell. Do you feel pleasure throughout your body? Would you like some nice instructions of further pleasure at this time?"

Mitchell nods.

"Officer Parks. Do you feel pleasure throughout your body? Would you like some nice instructions of further pleasure at this time?"

Parks nods his head.

"The robot in your custody, "Rufus", is innocent of any crime and in fact has assisted in the ongoing apprehension of the criminals and full recovery of stolen money. Remain seated. I will now exit through the rear door of this building. When you hear three knocks on the rear door, you will stand and walk slowly toward and on through the front door of this building."

Rufus then gives final instructions and tells both "I want you to the listen the music and begin dancing with your partner, arm in arm as you leave the building through the front door. When you hear your name called out by any person, you will exit your hypnotic trance and return to normal activity. You will not recall anything that happened during the state of your trance.".

Mitchell and Parks nod their head in understanding the instructions.

Rufus walks to the rear, opens the door and exits. He looks around in hopes of seeing Carl but, also to make certain he is clear to fully exit and leave the property. He then bangs on the door three times and walks away undetected.

Mitchell and Parks follow instructions and exit the front door of the building, closing the door behind them.

As they dance down the walkway toward the street, Mitchell begins to sing to the music they believe they hear. Parks joins him as they sing the song, "Forever, my love", while dancing toward the street.

A group of several police are standing outside the temporary command post listening to Captain Ramsey's update and further instructions. They hear singing from up the street as Mitchell and Parks dance. Sergeant Boyd glances over in front of the next building.

"Captain! Isn't that Mitchell and Parks?"

Captain Ramsey looks and then, responds. "What in the world are they doing?"

"Mitch, Parks! What are you doing? Where is that robot? Why are you dancing in the street, arm in arm? Have you boys turned gay?"

As Mitchell and Parks hear their name called out, they separate and stare at each other, then stare at the other group of officers.

"Where is that robot?" Captain Ramsey sends two other police running over to the building in search of Rufus.

Their quick search finds the building empty.

They yell back to Captain Ramsey. "The robot is gone. The building is empty!"

Captain Ramsey yells out to Mitchell and Parks as they stand steady in the street. "Go back to the station and wait! I will meet with you two later this afternoon!"

Radio communications have been ongoing and an updated announcement reports the vehicle that was described earlier by a neighbor has been stopped and both crooks apprehended along with two large bags of cash. Captain Ramsey gives the order to leave two officers at the scene to secure the site and everybody else can resume normal duties.

CHAPTER 10

Rufus sees Carl at a distance and calls out to him. "Carl!"
"Rufus!"
"Rufus, where have you been? I've looked everywhere
for you and became very concerned."

"Rufus is okay. I see your vehicle. Wait for me there. I must
make certain that Barbie Mergerint is safe with her dad. I will
then join you."

Rufus indirectly walks toward the temporary police command
center that was set up for hostage situation and robbery, still
staying out of sight to the police.

Once he has a good view of the area, he stops and steps behind
a police SUV to watch.

He sees five police exiting the building and then, Barbie
and her dad step out and walk to the SUV that transported Mr.
Mergerint to the scene. Rufus is happy now. He turns and walks
back to join Carl at his vehicle.

A well-dressed man approaches Rufus slowly and gently.
"Rufus, may I have a brief word with you?"

In the meantime, Carl thinks, "I'm calling Judy to let her
know all is okay. I'm sure she has been upset."

He dials her cell phone. It rings several times and then goes
to voice mail.

"Hon, Rufus is okay. We'll be home soon. Rufus has now gone back to the crime area to check on a person involved in the robbery. Everything is okay."

Carl stands alongside his vehicle and is constantly watching for Rufus. Finally, after several minutes, he strolls back toward the once tense area as he watches for Rufus.

Carl approaches a gentleman that stands near the crime area. "Sir, I came to this area with Rufus, a robot. Now, I can't locate Rufus. Have you seen him?"

"I've heard about your robot."

"And, I did see it a few minutes ago over near that dumpster. He then walked out of sight toward Beacon Street with two gentlemen."

"Okay. Thanks."

Carl trots down Whispering Pines Drive to Beacon Street. Looking around in all directions and no Rufus to be seen. He looks for anybody to ask if they that may have seen Rufus.

Now, what do I do? He thinks. Where is Rufus? Who were the two guys with him?

Carl is now in a panic stage. He needs to go home and see about Judy. Yet, he can't leave Rufus stranded here.

"Rufus! Rufus! Where are you?" he screams loudly as he walks back and forth on Beacon Street.

No response.

He thinks, "Now what the heck should I do? Maybe that gentleman has seen him again."

Back at the crime area, "Sir, have you seen the robot or his two accomplices yet?"

"No sir. I haven't seen anybody since you were here earlier. Sorry."

"Okay. Will you do something for me?"

"I'll try. What do you need?"

"The robot is called "Rufus". He came here with me and I must go home to check on my wife. I don't want to leave Rufus but, I must." If I give you my cell phone number, will you call me if you see Rufus and can get him on the phone to me?"

"Yes sir."

Carl writes his cellular number on the back of his store business card and hands it to the sergeant.

"I appreciate your help."

"I'll call you if I see Rufus."

As Carl hurriedly walks toward his car, he dials Judy's number again. No response. That is very unusual as Judy always has her phone within reach and quickly responds to his calls.

Carl is still frustrated and tense he drives away. His mind still racing through everything that has taken place. It's almost overwhelming.

Driving on Commerce Park Rd, "Woa. Oh crap! I almost collided with that car!"

He was so entangled with everything going on that his reduced concentration on driving almost caused a terrible wreck at the intersection.

As best he could, Carl concentrates on driving safely the rest of his way home.

Turning left and driving up the driveway, he engaged the automatic garage door opener.

"Aha. There's Judy's car. She's inside or, she may have left her cell phone on the bar and is working with her plants outside."

Inside the house, "Judy?"

No response as he opens the patio doors, "Hey Judy."

Quickly back inside he checks every room for any sign of her.

"She is not in the house, not outside, where in the heck is she?"

"Wait! Her phone is lying next to the kitchen sink! Something is wrong here!"

Quickly, he runs out through the garage to the house next door. In his panic state of mind, he doesn't even bother to knock on their door. He opens the door and enters, startling the neighbor.

"Anna! I can't find Judy! Do you know where she is?"

Still startled over his charging in her home unannounced, after a brief pause, Anna answers, "No Carl. I've not seen her."

"She is not in the house. She is not outside. Her car is inside and her call phone is inside the house. Now what else is going to go wrong today? I've got to find her. Will you help me?"

"Of course."

"You know what? Earlier this morning, I was in the office and happened to glance out the window. I did see her with two men. She got in the back seat with one guy. I thought that was strange."

"What kind of a car was it?"

"It was a large SUV, black with dark windows, probably a Cadillac Escalade." "Carl, you don't know where she was going in that SUV, or why?"

"No!"

"Oh my gosh. What are you going to do?"

"Anna, this is terrible! Something is wrong. And Rufus has disappeared with two men."

"Why? Where's Rufus? What's happened to Rufus?"

"I don't know. I'm sorry but, I've got to go. Call me if you see anything, anything at all. I've got to find them!"

Running back to the house, Carl's mind is in overload. "I can't call Judy. Her phone is in the house. I can't just wait for her to return. I've got to do something. If Rufus was here, between the two of us, we could come up with a plan, a solution to bring Judy back home."

"I've got to think straight and come up with something to do. This is terrible!"

He can no longer hold back the tears. Then, he goes down on his knees, faces the sofa and with elbows on the cushion he cups his head in his hands, still crying.

"Oh my Lord God Almighty, I need your help. My wife Judy is missing, she must be in some kind of trouble, maybe even kidnapped. Why? Lord. Why would anybody kidnap my precious wife? Oh Lord, I have learned to love You. Recently, I feel something special, like my spirit is connected to you. Until recently, I never even knew spirits were real. I never experienced spiritual love before I accepted your son, Jesus Christ as my Lord and savior. Please, God, as I lean on my spiritual connection with you, I pray that you will take care of Judy, keeping her away from any harm, and return her to me. I pray this prayer through your son Jesus Christ that died on the cross for our sins. Amen."

Carl stood up. His mind is now more focused, finally. First, he will call the sheriff's department with what Anna told him about the SUV.

Quickly, he looks up the phone number for the sheriff's department

"County sheriff's department, deputy Lawrence speaking, how may we help you?"

"I'm Carl Forcrast. My wife has been abducted from home. She's been kidnapped."

"What is your address Mr. Forcrast?"

"9012 Searmour Drive."

"What makes you think your wife was kidnapped?"

"When I returned home from a meeting, her car was in the garage, her cell phone on the counter, and she is nowhere around here. My neighbor said she saw my wife being led to a SUV, put in the back seat and they left. Can I get an investigator on this quickly? Please!?"

"May I put you on hold for up to two minutes, Mr. Forcrast?"

"Okay."

Carl is patting the table with his hand, patting his foot, all in response to his panic frustration.

"Mr. Forcrast, I am transferring this call to Lieutenant Blake. Please hold."

"Lieutenant Blake takes the call. "Mr. Forcrast, you believe your wife has been kidnapped?"

"Yes sir. She has been abducted."

"When was she abducted?

"I do not know. I left home at seven-ten this morning and returned about noon. She was here earlier and when I returned, she was not here."

"And a neighbor saw her being placed in an SUV?"

"Yes. Forced in the back seat."

"Mr. Forcrast, you own that A.I. robot we've heard about, don't you?"

"Yes."

"I'm going to place you on hold for just a few seconds and, I'll be right back. Okay?"

"Yes."

"Okay, Mr. Forcrast, lieutenant Boyce and Sergeant Lloyd are on their way to your home. They should be there within twenty minutes. Please stay home for their visit."

"Thank you, sir."

Carl is pacing the floors a four-door sedan pulls up the drive. "That must be the sheriff's department he thinks."

As the two deputies approach the front door and introduce themselves, Carl welcomes the two inside.

While Lt. Boyce talks with Carl, Sergeant Lloyd walks next door to gather information from Anna.

All during the questioning interview, Carl is busy thinking, "Why don't they do something? All these questions are not bringing her home. All they're doing is completing a lot of hand written notes on a pad. They'll never really do anything to bring Judy home."

At the conclusion, Lt. Boyce stands up and tells Carl, "Based on your information and that provided by Anna Wells next door, we do believe that it's possible that your wife may have been taken from your home against her will. Do you know of anybody that may have wanted, or had reason, to abduct her?"

"I do not."

"We're going to get on this very quickly. If you see or hear anything pertaining to the case, please call me immediately. Here is my card."

"I will do that. Please keep me informed on what you are doing and any developments"

"Yes sir. We'll definitely do that, Mr. Forcrast."

Carl walks to the living room window as the officers proceed to leave. They stop just short of opening the car doors and began talking to each other across the car top. "Probably discussing the next step in locating Judy", he thinks.

He is becoming more frustrated and scared as he tries to sort through all the events while pacing the floor.

"Judy is missing and needs my help. Did she willfully go off with the people or, was she forcibly taken? What if she is injured? And, what the heck is Rufus up to? And, where is that over intelligent piece of ram when I need him?"

"I've got to calm down and get a grip on this situation", he thinks as he seats himself in his favorite chair. But he then looks over at her normal, empty chair and jumps up again. That's too much of an expectation for her to be seated there. "I'm going to walk outside. Maybe she left a note or a clue for me."

"Did they exit through the garage? Anna did not say. But she probably went out through the front door because she didn't have the garage door opener with her and the door was closed. Come to think of it, the front door was not locked when I opened it earlier."

"I'll look outside first, then search inside the house."

He goes out through the front door, walking slowly for any sign, a piece of paper, anything that might indicate what is going on and, who she left with. Carefully scanning the walkway, drive-way, and grassy area produces no clue. Frustration still building as he walks back to the front door.

Inside, he continues to search for a clue. He thinks there may be some indication toward even a small clue. "Wait! I have not checked her cell phone laying here." Rushing to pick up the phone, he first scans phone calls for the day. He sees his calls to her and only one incoming call he does not recognize. The text messages are from friends that he knows. Back to the strange phone number listed, he decides to call it.

He enters the phone number and presses send. The phone rings four time and somebody answers, "Hello. Thanks for calling ACE Hardware. My name is Justin. How may I be of help to you today?"

"Oh Justin, I dialed the wrong number. I'm sorry."

"That's perfectly okay sir."

"Nothing is working! I'm not coming up with anything toward rescuing Judy. And, my confidence in the sheriff's department prompt work is very limited. I'm sure they took the paperwork back to the office and just filed it away. Maybe they alerted other officers to be on the lookout for any lady fitting Judy's description."

Doorbell rings.

Carl rushes to open the door!

"Hey Carl. My wife, Anna told me that Judy is missing, or something? What's going on?"

"Bret, I don't have a clue. This is terrible! Terrible! Come on inside."

"Probably doesn't mean anything but, I just got home from the office and I noticed a strange vehicle parked up the road and facing this direction."

"Really? Where? What did the car look like?"

"A black Chevrolet SUV."

"Really?

"Okay! Come with me, Bret. I want to check it out. Hurry."

Bret and Carl run through the house and into the garage. Carl presses the garage door opener on the way to his car. They get in Carl's car and he backs out.

As they leave the driveway and onto the road, Carl points to a dark SUV up the road in a distance. "Is that it?"

"It is. They are still in the same spot."

Carl is in a hurry but, proceeds in a normal speed. He doesn't want to spook anybody inside the SUV in his anxious state of mind.

"Bret, I hope this is the break I'm looking for. I pray it is."

They near the SUV and Carl pulls in close and rolls down his door glass. "Hey!"

A young lady opens her window. "Can I help you?"

"What are you doing out here?"

"I'm waiting on a friend to arrive home. Why does it matter to you?"

"I'm jittery and in somewhat of an emergency situation. I apologize to you ma'am."

"That's okay. I'm waiting for the Ratcliff family to come home. We're supposed to meet with them and go out for an early dinner."

"Thank you."

Carl pulls away and decides to make a few left turns circling the area, take the long way home. "Bret, I'm too emotional right now. Please overlook my tears."

"You go right ahead my friend. A good cry may help you gather yourself."

Silence as the drive places them back in Carl's garage. "Bret, come on inside. I just need a friend right now, and you're it."

"Absolutely."

Inside, Carl walks over and opens the front door, leaving the glass door closed. "I need to see out front in case we have a car approach the area."

"I understand. Have you reported this to law enforcement?"

"Yes. They were here earlier. I keep believing Judy will show up, or call. Today's weird happenings seem crazy to me. Rufus leaves with a stranger. I get home and Judy has apparently been kidnapped or, at least coaxed into leaving the house with strangers. This all so unbelievable to me."

"Your emotions could take over and alter your judgement. Try to remain as calm as possible. We'll get through this together."

"Do you believe the two cases are linked?", Asks Bret.

"That's a good question. It is odd that both have suddenly disappeared. But I don't see how they could be linked. It appears that Rufus left with a stranger of his own free will. Judy seems to have been abducted, or at least persuaded under duress. I know one thing. I'm at the verge of panic. But, I've gotta' maintain my sanity."

"Carl, I wish there was something I could do for you."

"You are. Just you're being here to share some of my anxiety and frustration is important. I appreciate it more than you could ever know."

Both, Carl and Bret are conversing and failed to see a vehicle turn onto the driveway and approach the house.

The doorbell sounds.

Carl jumps up and darts to the front door and wastes no time opening the door.

He recognizes Steve, a deputy sheriff and close acquaintance. "Steve! Please come in. This is one time I hope you are here on business."

"Carl, it's always good to see you. No, I happened to overhear part of your conversation with our dispatcher and thought I would see if there's anything I can do for you. Tell me what's going on."

"First of all, thank you for caring."

"Rufus and I were near the credit union hostage site earlier. When I was ready to leave, it's like Rufus simply disappeared. I found out that he had apparently left the area with a stranger, I came home to wait for Rufus only to find Judy missing. Next door neighbor, Bret's wife, Anna told me that Judy was taken away by two men in a black SUV. Beyond that, I know nothing."

"Okay. Carl, I'll do what I can for you, at least keep an eye out for a black SUV acting suspiciously in the area. I'll keep a keen eye out for Rufus, and for Judy as I patrol around the county."

"I appreciate that, Steve."

"You just stay calm. This will all work out. You'll be notified the minute we come up with anything in the case."

Steve leaves and Bret turns to Carl. "I believe everything is going to be okay. I just have that feeling, an extra sense we'll call it."

"Thanks. I appreciate your friendship."

"Bret, think hard. What should I do now? What can I be doing? All I'm doing now is pacing the floor. I walk outside and then come back inside. Every minute seems like an hour. This is terrible."

"I believe in prayer. Just pray. And, you're not accomplishing anything by pacing around. You may consider going over to your favorite chair and sit. Open your mind and convert away from worrying. Close your eyes. Take five deep, slow breaths as you totally relax your neck and shoulders. Then, just turn it all over to the Lord. Begin thinking of less stressful thoughts. Positive thoughts about how Judy is okay. She had her reasons for leaving with strangers and she's okay. She's talking to the strangers and listening, all to her benefit. She wants to be here with you as much as you want her. Only she knows the reason for all this and she is in control. She is in control of the situation and she's okay.

Silence.

"Bret, you're right. Worry accomplishes nothing. There is nothing I can do until something breaks in the case. Either the sheriff's department comes up with something, or Judy contacts me.

"Let's go out for a walk. Walking down the road and back may help me at this point. Any incoming calls about the situation will come in over my cell phone."

"Carl, that's a good idea."

Carl walks to the foyer closet, opens the door and picks one of his dozen or so caps to shade the sun from his eyes. "I like this military cap. Did you serve Bret?"

"I did. I was in the air force for four years".

"Me? I was in the U. S. Army. Best thing that could happen to me at that age. I emerged as a young man with character, strong work ethic, and eager to succeed in anything. My tour in the military made a man of me."

"Anyway, I'm proud to wear this cap with the U.S. Army insignia on it. Let's go. You ready?"

"Ready. I'm calling Anna to let her know where we're going."

Anna answers the phone. "Hello."

"Anna. Carl and I are going to exercise a bit by walking up the road. Call me if you need anything or, if you see anybody at Carl's house."

"Okay."

Bret senses that Carl is being unusually quiet as they begin walking. He sees that as good because Carl needs to think things through and probably doesn't need somebody blabbing their mouth right now. Carl walks along, at times he is looking down and other time looking off into the horizon, while quite obvious that his concentration is not on the horizon.

"Bret, what do you think is going on? You haven't said anything that may be taking place and involving Judy."

"Me? I'm not concerned. I told you before that I have like an extra sense about what is going on with Judy and I'm just not concerned. I'm, like you, anxious, a little concerned, yet I'm not worried."

"Okay. You're probably right, but I'm just too deeply connected, I guess."

"Carl, my friend, Judy will be okay. She will be okay."

Their pace down the paved road is slower than a normal "out for a walk" pace.

They are now about half a mile from their houses and approaching the railroad overpass.

"Why don't we sit down on these overpass concrete guards. I just need that open sky views to clear the cob webs from my brain, so to speak."

Carl sits, at first with legs pointed across the road toward the other guard. He then swings his legs around facing the train track below and with his legs swinging over the guard.

Bret joins him. He looks down at the tracks below. "Those tracks must be at least twenty feet below us. he thinks. People under a lot of pressure and worry can jump off a road, taking their life."

An approaching car slows and the driver waves as he passes by.

"Bret, I grew up in an area of the country with everybody speaking as they drive by you. When Judy and I first moved out on this road, nobody spoke to anybody. They just came home from work, went in their particular houses and neighbors never knew they existed until they went out the next morning."

"Now, a few years later, most everybody on this area of the road initiates a wave, or a "hello" to everybody they see."

Traffic is light to moderate with vehicles driving by as they go to and from their area homes. A horn sound as a car passes by. Both Carl and Bret turn quickly and respond with their wave. Bret has seen that car before but, has never met the owner. Light traffic continues with a car driving by every few minutes.

"Bret, I think I want to go back home, if you don't mind."

"Of course."

Bret gives one final look at the tracks and swings around to stand.

Carl is already standing. He stretches and begins a slow-paced walk toward home. Both move closer to the left shoulder of the road allowing plenty of room for an approaching vehicle from behind. As it goes by, everybody waves from the passing Cadillac sedan. Then another car is right behind it. A third car approaches and goes on by as Carl and Bret continue their walk.

Bret looks at his watch. "Carl, it's 5:15 pm and it's apparent that residents out here are coming home from work, with all this traffic."

"Yep."

They hear a vehicle stop behind them, probably to get a view of the railroad tracks and bridge. Another car blows their horn and proceeds to pass the stopped vehicle. Both Carl and Bret step completely off the pavement to make room for the passing car. They speak and wave as the car speeds on away, then Carl looks back at the other vehicle that had stopped and still partially in the road.

Carl looks closer. "Oh, my gosh! Oh, my goodness! screams Carl", as he springs toward that vehicle with its driver door glass partially down and a hand waving.

Bret turns. He reacts in full surprise, startled, and motionless. He does not know what is happening. Then he sees the vehicle door fly open and Judy springing toward Carl.

Both Carl and Judy are screaming in tears as they hug each other and exchange kisses.

Bret remains motionless and happy.

Carl backs up, looks Judy in her eyes. "I've been hysterical, like you wouldn't believe. Thank God, I'm so happy now. Seeing you is the answer to my prayers."

Still crying and can barely pronounce words, Judy wails out, "I knew you were worried

Still crying, "I knew you were upset and I couldn't do anything about it. Let's get in this car and go on to the house."

"Where did this vehicle come from? Why are you driving it?"

"I'll tell you as soon as I can catch my breath from this sudden excitement."

"Rufus? Do you know where Rufus is?"

"Carl, dear, Rufus is in the car. He's fine and so am I. I'll tell you about it after we get to the house."

Bret says, "Rufus, come up to the front passenger seat, okay?"

"You two emotional people get in the back seat and I'll drive home. I'm Calling Anna. She'll want to hear all about it."

The phone rings in and Anna answers. "Hello"

"Hon, we are with Judy and on our way back to their house. Be there in two minutes. Drop whatever you're doing and walk over. Okay?"

Through all the emotions, Rufus has remained quiet and motionless in the front passenger seat.

Turning in the long driveway, Anna is already standing near the garage. Bret pulls up near her and one by one they exit the vehicle.

Anna greets Judy with a hug. "You've had all of us worried sick. Welcome home. Hey, isn't this the same SUV you left in earlier?"

"Anna, that's a story within itself. Let's all go inside. I need a bottle of water, then Rufus and I will fill you all in."

Inside, Judy takes the lead with her water in hand. "Let's all go out on the deck. We can enjoy the outdoors while talking. Okay?"

Carl opens up the conversation. "How did you and Rufus end up together? Why are you driving that SUV, isn't it the same vehicle that you left home in? Have you been injured? Where have you been?"

"Hold up! Slow down, hon!"

"Just sit back and we'll go through the entire episode with you. Just listen. If you have any questions, hold them 'til the end and we'll discuss them at that time. Will you do that?"

"Rufus. You start with your part of this puzzle."

"A man approached me saying his associates wanted to talk with me. I refused. He then told me that Judy was a hostage and unless I complied, his associates would probably kill Judy.

Emotionally, that threat had no bearing on me. I made the decision to go along with them and unravel their plans, not to save Judy. So, I rode with the man. After twenty-seven minutes we arrived at a warehouse on the southside of town. I walked in and saw Judy, unharmed and free to move about as she wanted within the limited area provided. There was five other men. Two men were dressed in tailor made business suits. Three of the men were dressed casually in jeans, quite muscular in stature. Of course, our driver was dressed in slacks and nice shirt. All were very friendly, very cordial and obliging to a point."

"Judy, you take it from here."

"The description that Rufus gave, and their demeanor is good."

"The two men came to our house and persuaded me that both Carl and Rufus needed me immediately, especially Carl. One of the men told me that he is close friend of our medical doctor and that doctor Remick had summoned him to take me to Carl, that Carl had been injured at a place on the south side of town. They were so convincing that I agreed."

"I was concerned and scared as we left home and until we arrived at the warehouse and I saw Rufus. I felt easy with him nearby."

"Even after I discovered the hoax, those guys were so convincing, so nice, that I continued to just go along with their working with Rufus. Believe it or not, I felt Rufus could end up in control."

Rufus continues, "These men were foreign espionage agents. I will disclose the country they represent when I talk with federal authorities. These agents were dispatched here with orders to capture me and to learn everything I knew, my sources for the vast technical and international information that no other computer offers. There was electronic wave and detection equipment set up to determine my truthfulness as they commenced to question me. In reality, they were not very intelligent, not smart at all. Unknown to them, I could alter the interpretations and readings of the equipment. At first, they began asking me simple questions. The questions became more and more intense toward national and international security issues. I knew their mission had to be shut down."

Judy interrupts, "Rufus may I say something?"

"You may."

"Amazing. Simply amazing! Of the six men, one was seated directly in front and facing you. He was the point guy, asking questions. You could tell that he thought he had you totally under his control. The other five men began slowly backing away to different areas of the room. At first, I thought they were positioning themselves for something drastic!"

"I don't know how Rufus did it but, he placed each of those guys in a some sort of a trance, one by one. Toward the end, one of the guys seemed to notice something strange going on with his team members. He became very alert and seemed to be ready to spring into action. Then he calmed down. His eyes were staring away and he became calm and quiet. He was also immobile and in a trance. I believe he was the leader of that group. Once in a trance he walked over to one of the desks and made a telephone call. By this time, the last guy, an administrator that was working directly with Rufus sat down alongside Rufus in a stupor. I could see but, I could not hear what was being said by the team leader. He pulled out his wallet and seemed to offer a credit card during the conversation. Finally, he leaned back, staring off in the distance, as was the remaining four."

Carl asks, "Rufus, what was going on?"

"You'll find out shortly. It will all fit together."

Judy continues. "Rufus then turned to me, seated at a distance behind him. He instructed me to quickly walk out the door and wait near the SUV. As I walked out to the vehicle, behind me were the five men, all in a line and, with Rufus following."

Carl, Bret, and Anna are sitting motionless and absolutely quiet as they listened in total amazement.

"Rufus instructed those five to the seating arrangement. He then turned to me as I stood beside the left front wheel of the vehicle, "Judy, you drive and say nothing. I'll direct your route.""

"Carl, you can imagine the anxiety that I faced. I didn't know what was happening with those men, I was like a puppet, doing exactly as I was told, yet very scared that those guys would take over again and punish us."

"I was very cautious, overly cautions with my driving their rental Cadillac while following Rufus's instructions. He did program the destination in the vehicle GPS and that made it easier. Twenty minutes later I recognized our destination. We arrived at the airport entrance, not to commercial flights, but we were arriving at general aviation. Rufus summoned the office to open the security gate and instructed me to drive through. After about fifty feet inside the fenced area, I turned right and parked near a small twin-engine jet. Rufus looked at me and placed his fore finger vertically across his mouth, telling me to remain quiet. He stepped out and opened the rear passenger door while instructing one of the men to open the other rear door. He then motioned for the five men to get out. They followed Rufus to the plane and stopped. He had a brief discussion with the pilot and walked back toward the vehicle. The pilot took over and gave instructions for each man to enter the plane."

Bret remarks, "I don't understand. How did you persuade those men to follow your instructions?"

Rufus replies, "You'll understand shortly. Stay with us. As Judy said, I returned to the Cadillac SUV, a vehicle that had been rented by the group leader. We remained attentive and observant as the plane taxied out and took off. As the plane went airborne, Rufus looked at Judy for confirmation that she was now okay."

"But, how did you pull this off? Where were those men going?", asked Carl.

"Back at the building, Rufus hypnotized each of the men and then, instructed the team leader to order services of a private jet to fly them out of the area. That leader paid for the flight with his credit card that had unlimited credit available.

"Where were they going?", asked Bret.

"Their jet flight plan was filed for travel to New York City. At the J. F. Kennedy airport's nearby general aviation, they were to de-board and promptly board a chartered 707 for Paris, France."

Judy asks, Rufus, "When and how do they come out of the trance you had them under?"

"I thought you would never ask. As their plane was over the Atlantic, each of their cell phones go off. They will answer the call and my voice saying "Hello, have a great trip" that releases them from their trance and back to a normal state of mind."

Carl asks, "But they will panic and make the plane return, will they not?"

"Of course, they will want to return. But, As the team leader made reservations, his specific instructions for the pilot to allow nothing to interfere with their flight to Paris. Nothing!"

Anna looked at Judy. "Judy, you must have been terrified the entire time."

"Of course. Yet, I know Rufus and his abilities to overcome most anything so, I allowed him to do his thing."

Bret speaks to Rufus. "Rufus, don't you think those foreign agents will return to the United States and pursue you again, and using a different tactic."

"Probably not. As agents that failed their mission, they will probably be assigned to a different task. Replacements by their government will be trained and assigned. They will most likely come after Rufus again. After all my abilities to reach super secure data for America is very valuable to them."

Bret asks. "I'm curious. Just how much secret stuff do you know and, how in the world do you get it. And, aren't other robots doing the same?"

"Rufus has the ability to connect to intelligent bearing electronics, some reaching out to satellites and, with my absolute loyalty to the United States of America, I relay information to appropriate loyal decision makers. I also have medical and legal capabilities equal to and beyond that of professional humans. And, no other robots have my capabilities. I was, and am a unique test model."

"Unbelievable! I feel honored to even live nearby. Anna and I will try not to ever make you upset with us in any way", Bret laughingly remarks.

"I am so thankful that everybody is safe and unharmed. Judy, you should take the next two days in total relaxation. Rufus, you have a meeting tomorrow morning at the Bruno Center. Remember?"

"Rufus remembers."

Rufus looks at Carl. "That SUV is a rental and must be returned to Action Car Rental agency."

"Okay. I'll drive it to their lot and Judy can follow me."

CHAPTER 11

"Good morning everybody. I'm John Pearsthall with W0ZI News your hometown metro network. In response to your interest, I thank you for participating in this live presentation at the Bruner Center. We are also being broadcast through our station. Today's guest welcomes your questions and comments toward in-depth discussions about topics of your choice."

"Now, allow me to introduce Carl Forecrast. Carl is the owner of Rufus, the super intelligent robot that is our featured guest speaker today."

"Thank you, John."

"My name is Carl Forecrast. I'm here today with our robot, Rufus. You may have read or heard about Rufus. You will be able to observe Rufus as a highly intelligent computer stashed away in a humanoid style body"

"Rather than recognizing Rufus as "it", My wife and I see and prefer Rufus as "he", not "it".

"Rufus is quite amazing in every way. He has no emotions. He does not hate, does not love. He is loyal to a fault. Rufus can quote exact history. To any professionals out there, doctors, CPA's, attorneys, etc. Rufus can put you to shame with his deep knowledge of those professions so, you are welcome to embarrass yourself and try him."

"Now Rufus, come on up. The floor is yours."

"Thank you, Carl. Thank you, Mr. Pearsthall. And Rufus thanks you all for inviting me to speak, to bend your ear as humans say. My name is Rufus. As you may note, I look to you like you may expect a robot appear, along with a human appearance. I really wanted to appear totally as a robot but, I guess they wanted to mess it up and have me look a lot like you."

The engineer and the station staff laugh hardily.

"This morning, I will do more listening than talking. I want to hear your topics and feedback rather than discussing my own preferences."

"Please. Let us begin. I'm going to respond to your topics with what may be called "street smart" answers. In other words, I will avoid using highly technical or high-powered terms that may be beyond common knowledge. That is not to discredit you in any way, keeping it simple allows any less educated person on the air, and not present here today, to understand.

"So, let us begin."

"Rufus, my name is Autry. I'm well in my 70's and have experienced the best country, best economy, best of the best, so to speak. I am very concerned about where this country is headed. Tell me how I can deal with these concerns."

"Autry, I am not a fortune teller, nor am I a prophet. I do not know the future beyond my understanding of the book, you call bible. Are you familiar with the bible, Autry?"

"I am. There is a bible on a table in my family room at home. I'm not versed in the bible but, believe it is important and does have some meaning."

"I'm glad you do recognize the bible. That's good, Autry".

"Let's talk specifics. What upsets you about today's world?"

"Oh boy! Have we ever fallen? Everything was peaceful back a few years ago. Now, young people dress and act like tramps. They riot, burn, and kill as if they have no conscience."

"I have reviewed life in America throughout the last two hundred years and you're correct. People have changed dramatically. Basically, people once loved each other, they always waved and spoke to each other, they communicated, they dressed with pride in their appearance."

"Autry, you are of the age, you can see a movement among people in the United States. That movement began decades ago when Russia declared they would take over America from within and never firing a shot."

"Purposely dressing as common slobs reflects negatively on that person's self-image and unfortunately, it's programmed in their minds through education in public schools and forced into action by unions as prescribed by communism. Here's an example I have used before other groups, there is a movement to dress everybody down to rags, while lifting the image of politicians. It is a proven fact that the general public looks up to with admiration the well dressed individual, and that is laid out in planning by your country's political climate to position the "little people" so they look up to the well-dressed politician with extra respect. There was a time when church pastors always preached while wearing a suit and tie. Pastors are now persuaded to dress down and appeal to the lower self-imaged people"

"Next?"

Standing, "My name is Judith."

"Good morning Judith, what's on your mind?"

"We have a daughter in her second year of college. She is changing. She is caught up in pressure from other students toward socialism. She has been fighting the movement but, we can tell a difference that we don't like. Professors grade students for their leadership in demonstrating and destroying property. She seems to hold to our ways of raising her but, she seems to be drifting toward being a socialist."

"Thank you, Judith. So, let's look into the education system. Social liberalists believe that governments must actively promote freedom of citizens, and can only occur when government guarantees the right to education, health care, a nominal income, while enforcing laws against discrimination in housing, employment, clean air, and welfare, all funded by a huge taxation. Socialism began its' start-up in the early 1800's when Charles Fourier and others wanted to reorganize society toward cooperation and communion among people, stepping away from capitalism's competition in supply and demand. Under socialism, humans can still own property. Communism is different, as there is no private owned property. Communism in Soviet Union failed in 1991."

In the United States, the Socialist Party candidate Eugene Debs ran for president and received 6 percent of the vote. Socialism, in recent years has been identified between social democracy and communism.

Overall, communist countries have reduced in recent times as the world embraces free markets. China, Cuba, North Korea, Laos and Vietnam are communist because the government controls the entire economy, and their political system. Many North Koreans earn very little and exist on rations handed out by government. Again, Communism does not allow private property.

China is the economic power among communist nations. The compound that houses their leaders is behind a high wall and is heavily guarded."

"Sound familiar?"

"A German named Karl Marx became influential with his philosophy that the working class of people would take over the production of goods and erase all classes of people. Marx didn't clearly understand and differentiate communism from socialism."

"Socialism is preparing Americans toward Communism. One difference is that socialists can own property. Communism takes away that property, among other things. Once the country turns to socialism, it's then very easy to convert to communism. Socialism is being crammed down your daughter's throat and the universities are brain washing students on the topic. Students either agree with the movement or they may not receive a passing grade. China, Russia, and Saudi Arabia have already funded well over sixty billion dollars ($60,000,000,000.00) to the universities that promote socialism in students. Since the constitution, America has been the wealthiest, happiest, strongest nation in history. Other world powers that practice socialism and communism style governments have been jealous of America's financial, military, and Christian successes and will do anything to tear the United States apart. None have the military strength to change and control America. Governments that have turned to socialism now realize they are unable to revert back to a democratic government. Communist governments that include China, Russia, and North Korea are at a point of intent to become equal is to bring America down to their standard. Make sense?"

"Judith, you say that some college students contribute to their grades by demonstrating and destroying property. That again, is well planned. Communism was very envious of America's economy, health care, live styles, etc. since back in the 1950's. Khrushchev ruled over Russia and wanted to conquer America but could not win in a war. So, he announced to the world that Russia will overtake America and will never fire a shot, as in a war. Russia set out to change America from within. They planted professors in universities and paid them to teach Commune (Communism) survival and happiness as they began to lie about faults of capitalism. Over recent decades of teaching such propaganda, graduates emerge as brainwashed toward faults of capitalism. Today, a majority of politicians throughout the United States have sold out to communism and are turning against the greatness of America. Now, the problem goes much deeper and we'll look to that issue near the end of todays session. Rufus will guide you toward what can be done by you, and by all Americans, to render the adversities of today, as powerless. Listen closely and follow Rufus's plan. You may ask, how does this robot know the answer to our complex hate and political environment we face?"

"Just stay tuned."

"Judith, my recommendation is that you pull your daughter out of that university and place her in a college or university that is Christian driven. Those brainwashed socialist students emerging from colleges and universities today are America's future leaders. Unless the Communist infiltrated American education system is stopped and reversed, America, as you know it, is going to fall, and fall hard."

"Next topic?".

"Rufus my name is Parker?"

"Thank you for participating this morning, Parker."

"People spend their time on cell phones, texting. My nephew and niece visit us and they engage in absolutely no conversations with us unless we force it on them. They sit in our home with their cell phone in hand continually sending and receiving texts. They even send my wife, in the same room, a text asking about the next meal. I get so irritated to the point I almost tell them to leave and never come back to our house with their cell phone with them."

"Parker, I acknowledge your frustration. "People do spend too much time on cell on their phones. Let's peek at the bigger picture. There is a movement to disrupt the human-to-human interaction. In other words, if people stop communicating verbally and emotionally, and depend on written words only, they are easier to influence and to control in any mass situation by government. Again, as you heard earlier, it's all intentional and part of the bigger take-over of your freedom."

"On to the next level and influence, people are going to influenced by the mis-information they will be exposed to on their electronic devises. Here's an example, you see people carry and reference their electronic devise to follow the pastor's message during church, and no bible present."

"What's the intent? Church goers are being introduced to a smaller, handier reference to the bible. Why is that? As more Christians turn to electronic bibles, the bible words, phrases, as you know it is going to changed, very slightly, until you will no longer need a printed bible in your home. Even pastors are already beginning to open their electronic tablet instead of the book."

"Okay, let's allow the lady that is standing on this front row to speak up."

"First of all, I'm Marge and I want to thank Rufus for participating in this meeting."

"Well, thank you, Marge."

"My ongoing problem is that our daughter, age 29, has gained about fifty pounds over the last five years. She is fat! What can I do?"

"Does she cook her own meals? What does she eat?"

"No. She eats out at fast food shops most every meal and, spends her evenings on her electronics while snacking on potato chips and other snacks."

"Eating fast foods, three meals per day and when she goes shopping, her cart is full of potato chips and other snacks?"

"You've got it. You have identified the solution. Congratulations Marge."

"Take a moment and visualize your daughter gaining another hundred plus pounds. That's what she will weigh if she keeps up her horrible eating habits. And, you ask what can you do? Nothing. Only she can correct her weight problem. She must become motivated. You're motivated to help her but she is not motivated. Make sense?"

"A high percentage of younger people do not cook meals. They eat three meals daily at fast food restaurants. Now, why is that so fattening? The sugars, carbs, and spices mixed in and influence the flavor of fast-food meals are designed to create a craving to return for the ongoing meals at the same restaurant. I find it hard to refer to them as restaurants. They are a just a simple food shop. Those foods are a promoter of weight gain and, fast food shops are terrific marketers. They want your ongoing business so they add taste habit forming additives and chemicals to their foods. As you go to McDonalds for their sandwiches and fries, you become addicted to their foods, not their competitor foods. Nothing else can satisfy your craving, even a good home cooked hamburger and fries."

"I understand, Rufus. I will say that she has now joined a physical training program at a gym. Maybe that will help her."

"Not really. Not beyond short term. Government is not going to share this information with you. There's too many dollars and tax revenue involved. Your daughter may tone her body and appear leaner during work outs. She must change her eating habits. Working out at a gym can tighten muscle mass and cause her to be slimmer, actually losing fat. However, once you perform those strenuous exercises to accomplish trimming, you must continue exercising and increase the movements as you go for the rest of your life. In other words, working out to lose fat doesn't work. Proper food intake, compared to walking toward maintaining muscle strength in the heart, lung, legs and arms is the only way."

"Wow."

"And, let me provide an example. Carl has lost weight from 204 to 169 in seven months, very gradually. Changing eating habits for twenty-one days is the key. After twenty-one days, you no longer crave or want the old foods. Five days weekly, Carl eats either two boiled eggs, or a bowl of oatmeal for breakfast every week day. He eats a finely chopped salad of romaine lettuce, tomato, apple, celery, and other veggies with broiled chicken cubes and his homemade vegetable soup. He prepares the salad for 5 days consumption at a time. He walks three to five days weekly for one mile. He makes his own vegetable soup into freezer containers, enough for about two weeks at a time. His vegetables are frozen and he rinses them before cooking. He adds tomato sauce, cubed and broiled chicken breast to the cooker. On weekends, he may stray from this routine and eat normal meals, in moderation. Following Carl's eating habits, over time, can cause a person to reach their intended weight, based on their height

"Oh my. Thank you!"

John speaks up, "Rufus, will you take a few minutes to address politics in our country. Any political topic you wish. It seems some listeners are becoming reserved in expressing their beliefs in public. I wonder why that is."

"I will."

"People sense danger in expressing their political beliefs with others is growing. Why? People can already feel the grips of socialism, communism, and government control over what people say, where they live, how they live, and are afraid of the consequences."

"Politics has turned to lies. Lying is not only perfectly acceptable, but lying is okay and must be done in order to reach most elected politician's goal. They lie and the media knowingly backs up false news, even to the point that truthful witnessing of the lie is eliminated from news altogether. Truth is fast becoming a thing of the past anymore. There is a movement promoting lies. It's okay to lie. That is becoming the popular way in America. You know a time within a few years ago that your word was pridefully your bond. That again falls into the education systems teachings. It's okay to persuade others and lie to get your own way."

"Your government is on a mission, well planned, to control everything Americans do. Some controls are good. Recent electronic achievements allow your in-home conversations to be monitored. Certain words in any language flags, and engages massive computer systems located in a large federal facility to listen in on sentences that surrounds that particular word. Everybody's voice is unique. Your fingerprints are on file in a federal agency, so is your voice. Your cellular and other electronics, including most wrist watches, track your every move."

"Beyond Government, human minds have conquered simple electronics, elementary and simple compared to Rufus, but toward manipulating financials. Most everything you rely on for a better life is being manipulated by others toward their own gain in most cases. So, you're doing well with your stock investments? They are being manipulated toward capturing your money at the pre-designated timing."

"Rufus, I am doctor Covington. How do you know that what you are telling us is for real? I may not believe you."

"Dr. Covington, that's okay. You may or may not understand my abilities to reach into applicable systems and retrieve higher knowledge, much higher than you can even imagine. Let's take a brief look at your profession. Medical doctors are among some of the highest paid professions, specifically in specialized fields of medicine. Doctors have gained financial growth by charging for their services and then, charging for the specific room or, "facility" used to perform their services. You have no doubt been exposed to a new financial enhancement such as "materials charge". Your profession is looking at charging patients extra for examining table covers, needles, tape, etc. all bundled into a surcharge. Going to your office for an injection may involve a $40 insurance co-pay, $150 facility fee, and materials surcharge of $30. So, your patient normally pays forty dollars and their insurance picks up the balance. Now, the patient pays you $220 and the insurance provider still pays the same as always."

"Dr. Covington, has Rufus established your belief or, I can go into details of your kick-backs, or commissions from prescription orders? Then, there is the unnecessary surgical referrals kick-backs from surgeons? Shall I continue, doctor?"

Silence.

"Rufus, my name is Bret."

"Open up to me, Bret."

"I have heard your reference about people down dressing. You are comparing today's dress code to that of a couple of generations ago. Right? Well, things change. I'm twenty-five years old and the dress code you are picking on is the style among young people in this era. Young people that are much more intelligent than those old farts in this stupid country! And, you're falling into that same trap of stupidity. All those old people want is money, money, money. They are greedy and don't want to share with other people. In reality, I should, someday, have the same income and wealth as your owner, Carl."

"There is a much bigger picture directing that code. It's all about purposely dressing down. There is a game plan in motion."

"Hey Rufus, you're crazy! We, the upcoming leaders of this country, about to be the old country when we change it, will balance out all the wealth and medical needs in this country as we show the rest of the world how great socialism can be!"

"Okay "Brat", we hear you loud and clear. You are among the *humans that fail to see what they see*."

"Can you feel that rumbling in the floor beneath your chair? That's Satan grabbing for you. Hand on. You'll enjoy the ride until the everlasting, burning crash. But, that's okay. Just enjoy your journey now and you can beg and scream for help when the final stage is in place."

"Now, let's hear from a senior citizen that can share the change in times."

A gentleman raises his hand. "Rufus, my name is Madison Newberry. I've been around almost 80 years and can probably fill a slot as a senior."

"Well, thank you sir. Tell us your name a little louder, please."

"Madison Newberry. My wife calls me "Mad," he responds in a humorous tone." A few low laughs are heard across the audience.

"Okay."

"Great. Thank you, Madison. You and I are going to engage in some conversations about events and experiences of your past. Is that okay?"

"Sure."

"Madison, we want to hear you discuss your early years. If you will share some experiences that reflect people's happiness, or lack thereof, when compared to these years and times. Will you do that?'"

"I'm not certain I understand what you are expecting, but If you'll guide me, I'll certainly try to provide a view of the good years, compared to today's world."

"As a young lad in the fifties, I remember a neighbor's house burned down. Area neighbors within a three-mile radius came together with their hammers and saws to contribute in the re-building of that house. Dink Belew owned a sawmill nearby and he contributed the lumber. Getting a county permit to build the house was as simple as taking some rough sketches of the house for an instant approval. Area wives cooked and fed the builders as they spent day in and day out completing the dwelling. It was quite a sight."

"At times, a dozen or more neighbors contributed their time and skills. At other times, only three or four men would be on site. In a short time, the house was completed and the Henton family moved in. The Hentons' probably paid little to nothing for their new home."

Rufus says. "Thank you, Madison. Now, fast forward that event to today. Tell us how that same need would be dealt with today."

"No comparison. Today, that family would be on their own. Home owner's insurance would be their only hope. The process of getting a building permit could take several weeks of nit pickin', back and forth, as the local governments seem to make it as tough as possible, and slow as they can be. As I heard somebody mention, it's part of a government effort to control the people. Neighbors re-building the house, free of wages, and out of the kindness of their heart? Not today."

"Thank you, Mr. Madison. How about your happiness as a young man, compared to what you see in young people of today?"

"I was an only child on a big farm. We were up early and worked until dark. It was hard work. It was tough. However, I didn't know it was tough because I had no comparison to consider. When people went to church, they put on their best. Men and boys wore a suit and tie. No exceptions. Now, what I see today is a lack of pride in young people. They don't seem to have pride in the way they look, or in their ambitions."

"I watch my grandchildren as they continue to mature. My grandson doesn't know how to drive a nail. My sixteen-year-old granddaughter doesn't know how to boil water, much less cook anything. They illustrate an expectation for everything free, without payment or effort. Their only pride is in playing games on their computers and electronics. With that mindset, as they have grandchildren of their own, what will be their prideful achievement? They will have no comparison and, they will be totally satisfied as a dependent on government meek hand-outs."

"Thank you, Mr. Madison."

"Next?"

"My name is Lucy Stroffel. I am a high school teacher."

"Lucy, please tell us what's on your mind."

"Our education system sucks! I have eleventh grade students that can't calculate simple math. Their English language is mingled with no-nonsense words. Science is an unknown subject to them. We are required. I repeat, required to pass the students based on occasional attendance to the class room. That's all!"

"My husband, Joe, studied the near perfect resume' of a college senior. His resume did not have a cover letter attached. Joe asked him to prepare a cover letter and bring it to the scheduled interview. The resume was perfect because it was undoubtedly prepared by a professional resume service. The cover letter was the applicant's own preparation. That resume cover letter was unacceptable. He brought it home for me to read. Wording made no sense and spelling was that of a fourth grader. His resume presented him as educated in a local university and he couldn't spell words or form sentences that made any sense."

"Thank you, Lucy".

"Rufus, my name is Calvin, Calvin Mach. My wife and I have three children, a daughter and two sons. We're Christians and very conservative. My son, Jeffrey just graduated from a university and he is now against everything we have always protected in this country. Jeffrey no longer believes in any earthly creations as Godly. He believes government should provide everybody with free food, housing, and medical and that taxing corporations will pay the bills. He is brainwashed. He hangs out in our home, consistently on his computer playing games and goes through the motion of applying for a job. I can't get through to him. I heard this concern earlier but, what can I, we as a family do?"

"You are right. And there is an underlying force, a force that humans are not understanding. There is something that you can do, something very simple that all people can do to, at a point in time, calm down all the turmoil. I'll explain. I had intended to share the solution in this session, but our time is up."

From the back if the room, a man rises, holding his hand in the air, "Hey, wait just a minute. I have a question."

"Yes. Go ahead, sir. Quickly, please."

"My grandpa used to tell us about some politician that was President of the United States for one day. I never paid attention to such stupid comments but, he swore by that statement. Do you know anything about it?"

"Thank you, sir. In 1848, James K. Polk was the outgoing President. President elect Zachary Taylor was to take the oath of office that same day, Sunday, March 4, 1849. President elect Taylor refused to take the oath on the sabbath day. A law dated March 1, 1792 provided for any case of both the President and Vice President were unavailable, the President of the Senate Pro Tempore shall act as President. David R. Atchison was President for a day and President Taylor became President of The United States on March 5, 1849. Your grandpa is a smart and wise man."

John Pearsthall appears. "Rufus. Carl. We appreciate your taking the time to be on my show today this morning. This concludes our segment. We'll take a fifteen-minute break and return to Jerry Haghs' show, still in this Center. You may stay for his show, and if you do need to leave, a crowd is gathered outside, hopeful for an empty seat inside."

CHAPTER 12

Jerry Haghs walks out to the podium, "This Convention Center seats just over six hundred people and today we are completely full. If standing room was allowed by the fire code, we'd probably have over 800 people in attendance."

"You've all heard about Carl and Rufus and, this morning, it is my distinct pleasure to introduce Carl Forecrast who will in turn, introduce Rufus!"

"I thank you Mr Haghs"

"Good morning everybody. My name is Carl Forcrast. You have no doubt heard of Rufus, the overly intelligent robot. I tell Rufus that he has a warped intelligence." The audience laughs as they notice Rufus's expression to that remark.

"Rufus is here to share some of his "smart aleck" feedback on your subjects. "Normally he would like to discuss topics in a highly-technical manner, most of which we would not understand, so his answers and discussions will be what we might call a street-smart presentation. That probably upsets Rufus because he does like to show off his intelligence."

"You were asked to bring three discussion topics to this meeting. That's in case your topic is already discussed here this morning. You will have back up topics. As Rufus recognizes you, please stand, state your full name, a short topic that you wish to hear a response from Rufus."

"Now, I want to introduce our key note speaker today, Mr. Rufus, our hometown robot."

"Thank you, "Mr." Forcrast!". You should now be seated and shut up, is Rufus's response to the introduction, again, all in fun.

"We'll begin now as any of you begin with a subject you want to bring before the group. I, Rufus, stand before you as a simply devise, a machine if you will, with some extraordinary computer driven intelligence. Rufus has no emotions, very loyal to the truth and to the point that I am incapable of lying."

A man of about 30 years of age stands. "Rufus, my name is Billy Bikki."

"Thank you, Billy. And what is your subject up for discussion today?"

I vote as a democrat. I've been a democrat ever since I sat on my grandpa's lap and listened as he shared the benefits of democrats from the time, he was a teenager. Democrats passed laws that favored the people, not the politicians. They were for the people. Democrats are for people like me. Republicans take care of the big guys, the corporations and their executives. We forget that socialism is what took care of the everyday working man in those days. Republicans were riding their stock pile of assets and gave nothing to needy."

"Billy, you are correct as it applies to the 1930's and 40's, except the republicans are on record as more helpful to the welfare of those in need. Now, your democrat party of those days began to change in the 1950's. At that point, Republicans became the most supportive of advancing the working man, advancing him on to a prideful and meaningful financial growth and well-being. Democrats began to become more reliant on government hand-outs and dollars in the politician's pocket. Democrat politicians began to see that hand-outs could be productive in persuading, or buying votes."

"Stay with me, Billy. This gets deeper. In the 1950's after the Korean Conflict, democrat politicians became the target of influence by the Soviet Union, "Russia". On November 18, 1956, The Russian leader, Nikita Khruschchev, the first secretary of the

Communist Party of the Soviet Union declared on November 18, 1956, *"we will take America without firing a shot. We will bury you from within"*. Khruschchev was jealous of the American military power, financial power, and influence over the world as a whole. Russia could not identify any means to conquer America by traditional means. The Soviet Union established a long-term goal to bring America down. They quickly began feeding dollars into recruiting college students to become teachers and professors, and brain washing those influential recruits against capitalism and teaching socialism, the next phase toward communism. They were very selective in recruiting. Since the 1950's those recruits have become your politicians, corporate executives, and even demonstrators and rioters. Remember, the young brainwashed students are America's future leaders.

From across the room, "No! RoughHouse! You are making that up. I know for a fact that none of what you say is true!"

"And what is your name?"

Screaming out, "I am Selma Witistone! And you are a dummy that has been programmed to mislead the people into a fantasy belief! You are crazy. If I had a gun, I would put you away forever."

Rufus calmly responds, "My sources of information are real and reliable beyond any questioning."

"No! Absolute craziness on your part."

Rufus continues. "Selma Witistone. Selma may I interrupt you with question?"

"What?"

"Are you educated locally? In this city?"

"No! I attended a university."

"I see. Bear with me quietly for up to a minute, please"

Rufus seems to look off in a distance. His eyes not focused on anything in particular.

"Witistone. Selma. My review of records, sees that you, Selma J. Whitistone are educated. On September 3 last year, you organized a sit in with twenty-seven other people against Christianity. On March 12, you were arrested for prostitution and released on five-hundred-dollar bond. On April 9 you were arrested for possession of cocaine. July 4, you were identified as one of four people that threw packs of lit firecrackers into an occupied church meeting."

"Selma, you may now find some reason to believe any information Rufus may provide on any topic and expect that information to be absolutely flawless. Will you agree? Or shall I reveal records of your past that will be embarrassing to you?"

Silence.

Selma is looking to her left, toward a wall. She is mad. There is no response. Then, she quietly rises and is leaving the room through the rear exit as Rufus calmly tells her. "Selma, I mean no embarrassment to you and would in fact like to hear more of your beliefs. Please call the number on your registration. I would like to learn from you."

A well-dressed man, probably in his mid forty's stands and announces, "Socialism in America allows everybody free rent, free food, free medical. There is nothing wrong with that! In fact, we should all look forward to socialism."

"May we have your name, sir?"

"Harvey Prothewt."

"Mr. Prothewt. Please continue. How will the freebies be paid for?

"The government will provide everything. Taxes from those big corporations will pay for everything and more. In addition, we can reduce the national debt to zero in just a few years. Can't you understand that?"

"I have a vision, Mr. Plastek. Under socialism, I see the free food, free rent, free medical that you are talking about and all being paid by big business. That is until big businesses quickly decide to relocate out of the country. Then, government takes over some remaining corporations and attempts to greedily manage them. You should study Cuba. Cuba was once a thriving country. Today, under its iron hand ruling. People were kicked out of their nice homes and cramed into ultra-small apartments while Fidel Castro's hand-picked supporters then took over homes.

Mr. Plastek, you are young enough to see the same take-over in America. Who then suffers? You do."

"You're wrong. That will never happen. The constitution is outdated. It doesn't apply to today's needs."

"Really? Socialism has been tried by many countries and has never worked. Even Israel tried socialism for a short span. In January 1983, the socialism bubble burst and thousands of private citizens, businesses, and government entities faced bankruptcy. United States President Ronald Reagan offered $1.5 billion and Israel abandoned socialist's rules and adapted a U. S. style of capitalism."

"Finally, socialism is fatal conceit: The belief is that your government, under socialism can make better decisions for the people than people can make for themselves."

Standing with her hand in the air, Rufus recognizes the lady. "Thank you for participating. May we have your name?"

"My name is Christine. I grew up in a tough situation and learned to work early in life, just to help support my mother and brothers. Today, I see laziness throughout our community. They don't know the importance of pride in work. What can we do?"

"Christine, that's a great observation. Unfortunately, people no longer see a need to learn as many skills as you know. And, they will be okay. A grown man may not know how to drive a nail in a board, or even how to hold a hammer. However, most young adults today pay attention to their own trained skills and compensate others that are skilled for the work needed at the time."

"I see. I had never looked at it from that angle."

"And now the next topic."

"May we have your name?"

"I'm Paul. Do unidentified Flying Objects with extraterrestrials exist?"

"Thank you, Paul. Absolutely, they do. You won't hear that answer from governments and, I sense that Rufus's answer startled you. There were almost six thousand sightings reported in 2019 in America." Has anybody in attendance ever seen a UFO?"

"Yes. My name is Lance. I was in Quebec City, Canada last year admiring the architecture and taking pictures. I snapped three pictures of two buildings. When I uploaded the photographs onto my laptop, the middle pic definitely had a large disc shaped UFO hovering between two buildings. I guess it was not visible by eye, only camera lens."

"My name is Pete. Several years ago, a friend reported that he was traveling late at night along a two-lane highway. His vehicle radio began fading in and out while overhead became all lit up. He thought an airplane was flying over him with lights flashing. All at once, an object appeared as it flew out in front of his car and then landed partially on the pavement and partially on the shoulder. He slammed on his brakes and stopped, in a panic. He opened the door and stood with one foot on the pavement and the right foot still in the car. He said two beings, about four feet, eight inches tall, white hair, dressed in a silver covering that was gathered at the neck, wrists, and ankles, yet extended out over the feet and with much longer fingers. He reached inside the car for his firearm and they turned back. He said that within about three seconds, they were aboard the craft and flown out of sight. The next morning, he was to meet a television crew at the scene. I rode with him for that meeting. At the scene, there were two tire skin marks, narrow tire marks that would match his Volkswagen tread. The grass on side of the road was matted down in a circular pattern, matching his description of the U.F.O. as similar to half a football, cone shaped. He definitely saw something, alive and strange to humans."

"Thank you, Pete. People need to recognize that extraterrestrials are part of your God's plan. They do exist. There are more than one species representing other solar systems and mean no harm as they study our backward ways. In fact, they have played ESP roles to humans in guiding you to new inventions and ways to improve this planet and its people."

Rufus adds, "A state of Georgia politician was traveling along interstate seventy-five. He and other drivers observed a UFO flying low and setting down nearby. He and several vehicles pulled on the side of the highway to observe. That politician, Jimmy Carter later ran for president of the United States and was elected. While campaigning, Jimmy declared that when he became elected, he would share all information about UFOs to America. Once elected, he was advised to say nothing. Unidentified flying objects, space ships, if you will, do exist. They too, are God's beings.

"Anybody else?"

"I'm Joel Hangroven and I would like to join with you in a discussion about the New World Order."

"Joel, I'm aware of the subject. Rather than a joint discussion, why don't you provide us with your review of N W O."

"I can do that. John D. Rockefeller III's Population Council, the World Band, and others have been working with the World Health Organization for over 20 years to develop an anti-fertility vaccine using tetanus and other vaccines. The plan includes scientifically engineering the global population. The propose cutting the world population to less than one billion from its almost eight billion."

"As the NWO pertains to the United States, a planned approach to use American money and know-how to establish competitors, while at the same time use every devious strategy to weaken and impoverish this country. The goal is not to bankrupt the United States individually. It is to reduce our productivity, and our standard of living, to the meager subsistence level of the socialized nations. At a pre-arranged time, a country will announce its insolvency. Following that announcement, the domino effect spreads as other countries declare bankruptcy on each other."

"Thank you, Joel. I may add the fact that certain U. S. politicians are playing in to the NWO and desired roles. They see that by the year 2035, the NWO plans to become a fully global governing body with its leaders coming from countries that have experience in controlling their people, leaders in climate control, full military control of its population. United States politicians see the opportunity and, see the opportunity to be a fore runner in the overall NWO Policies and world control. The aggressive politicians with the experience hope to be promoted to a world governing position when the time comes."

"Rufus, if I may add to the discussion, there is another group playing its role of the NWO. The Trilateral is group of successful men representing North America, Western Europe, and Japan-hence the term "trilateral". The group remains secretive, yet it is known, the people, governments, and economics of all nations must serve the needs of multinational banks and corporations and control over economic resources, all with its power in politics."

"Thank you."

Standing, waving her arm. "My name is Pinkie. I'm LGBTQ, specifically, I'm lesbian."

"Your name is what? Pinkie?"

"It is."

"Pinkie. We're all thankful that you are not one of those go for it all transgenders. At least we know you have something down there."

Brent stands up and screams, "Everybody listen! If Rufus doesn't inspire you, nothing will." Go "*Rufie.*"

Pinkie looks around the room and quickly establishes she has no support and is probably the only person of her culture among the crowd. She calmly sits down.

Rufus continues, "Pinkie, Rufus is picking on you, all in fun. You have something to say?"

Silence.

"Audience, you are being bombarded with information today that can be concerning, somewhat scary but, I know the great results you would like to hear. I will share exactly what can be done that turns the tide on your issues. Just stay with me. There is a simple solution for everybody, a solution that has yet to be emphasized in the terrible consequences lying ahead."

"Next, please."

"Yes, Rufus. My name is Willard. I would like a discussion about that God I hear so much about."

"Thank you, Willard."

"Let's begin with some audience experiences. Heaven or hell? If you have had God's intervention that saved your life, stand up and tell us about it."

Standing, "My name is Carl. I was involved in an automobile accident and was transported to the hospital. X-rays and a scan of my neck area revealed a small spot on my left lung. I had my pulmonary doctor look at the scan and, because I had been examined six months earlier and the spot was not visible, he believed it to be a nodule caused by the seat belt. Shortly thereafter, it was identified as cancer, recent and less than half inch in size. The top half of my lung was surgically removed. I had no chemotherapy, no radiation as follow up. I can tell you the Lord set up the accident so I would detect that cancerous cell early and before it could affect my life span."

"Rufus, my name is Gerald."

"I was flying with a friend, the owner of a Mooney 201 single engine airplane. We took off from the Macon, Georgia airport. The plane was trimmed out, automatic pilot was engaged, and in a smooth climb. At about forty-five hundred feet, the plane engine sputtered, the propellor flared out, and we went into a power glide. Mayday alerts were sent out on the radio and the Macon tower asked if we could get back to the airport. My friend replied that we would try. The air traffic controller stopped all air traffic, in and out, and advised us to take any runway we could get to. Mechanics could not identify any cause for the engine failure. We decided to go airborne again. As we taxied down the runway, building speed and the plane began to feel soft on the runway as it does just before you pull back on the yoke to go airborne, the engine sputtered again. The pilot immediately shut down airborne attempts. If we had gone airborne, even ten or twenty feet in the air and the engine shut down, we would have been splattered all over the runway. God was protecting us! Why? The Lord must have a mission intended for us. At a later date, the friend was flying the plane over a forest area and the engine slung a rod through the side of the engine. He had no power, no electrical that would allow him to lower the landing gear, and the cockpit filled with smoke. He crash-landed the plane on a strip of narrow road and survived."

"Next?"

"My name is Button.... I'm called Button because my dad first saw me and said, "he's cute as a button". There was laughter throughout the room in response to his comment. "I was driving on two lane highway, kinda' out in the country traveling eastward from Lake City, Florida. The established speed for the highway was fifty-five miles per hour. I had some job-related paperwork laying in the passenger seat and reached down to briefly pick up and review a form. In doing so, I lifted my foot off the gas pedal and slightly applied the brake, slowing my car as a safety precaution. As I lay the paper back in the seat and set my eyes back on the highway ahead, a pickup truck ran a stop sign and sped across the highway about fifteen feet in front of me. I then fully applied the brakes, pulled to the side of the highway and took a few long breaths as I thanked God for his protection."

"Wow! Those are some stories that will make you appreciate your God, am I right?"

The audience clapped.

Rufus continued. "Rufus would like for volunteers to keep this topic going, anything about your God that will be fulfilling to the others. As you know, as a robot, I have no soul, no spirit, and I wish I did."

"Rufus, you're so intelligent, so just where is God."

"Maybe you will find out someday. From a simplistic standpoint that I can relate to you so you will understand, here goes. When you walk outside at night, you look up and see the moon with uncountable numbers of stars along with planets. You know the sun will be visible during daylight and that earth and other planets are revolving around the sun. These stars and planets, including earth are part of this solar system. That's all you can see. Let's look deeper and visualize other solar systems just outside yours. Other beings are assumed to live in other systems. Those other beings may be extremely more intelligent that you are. God is in that mix and is most intelligent of all, intelligent beyond human understanding. You expect Rufus to point directly to the location of God. Rufus is far too simple to even attempt. Thank you very much."

Rufus speaks, "We'll take a fifteen-minute break now. Rufus needs to pee."

Several giggles filled the room.

"When we convene, we'll address some written notes from you all. So, please take a blank index card from the registration table and note any topic details you want to have addressed. Then place the completed card back on the left side of the table."

The meeting breaks as some head for the water and soft drinks as other just visit with each other. In the hallway, Rufus is surrounded with those wanting to just meet a robot. Others have questions and viewpoints that generally are of the topics at the meeting but, meaningful for the most part.

As the break time nears an end, everybody makes their way back to the meeting room. Rufus follows and picks up the completed index cards from the table.

"I want to thank each of you that participated and completed these registration cards. I hope we'll have time to go through each one. So, let's begin."

"This card says, only 144,000 people are going to heaven. I doubt if I can do anything to get there."

"My answer to this concern is that the one hundred fourth four thousand applies to the twelve tribes of Israel of which you are part to."

"Next card reads, "Must I join a church in order to get to heaven?"

"No. You must live according to God's word that you'll find by studying the bible.

Attending church will place you among others that love the Lord and exposes you to a stronger Christian understanding that leads you to loving Jesus Christ, your savior."

"What about Muslims? Will they go to heaven?"

"Some may. It depends on their acceptance of Jesus Christ as their savior, not simply a prophet."

"Allow me to arrange these cards. I see a few that the same basic answer may apply."

"Man lived in a whale for three days?"

"One fish fed thousands of people?"

"Cambridge researchers discovered they have pinpointed the date of the biblical account of Joshua, through God, stopping time to a stand-still on October 30, 1207 BC. The eclipse helped pinpoint reigns of Pharaohs Ramesses and Merneptah."

"God can and does perform miracles, as they may appear to humans. He is the All Mighty. It may appear to be magic, but it's not. It's God. Making time stand still may, and Rufus will declare "may", have accounted for man remaining in a whale for three days."

"He may have caused the boy with one fish and one loaf of bread to feed five thousand people, again by causing time to stand still while more fish and bread becomes available."

"Jesus turned water to wine? How?"

"Again, making the time stand still could allow for the seemingly impossible feat."

"The next question is, who is Satan?

"While Satan is the formidable enemy of God, we must always remember that he was defeated and cast out of heaven along with his supporting angels. He has angelic powers, but Jesus is all-powerful."

A young man on the front row interrupts, asking, "Where is God?"

"And what is your name?"

"Lonnie."

"God exists in his kingdom referred to as Heaven. Spiritual God is present in the mind and love of persons that reach out to and accept his spirit with their love."

"So, God lives within me?"

"Yes and no. God's spirit lives only in the heart and mind of those that know, accept, and love him."

"Are you saying that because I have never reached out to God, have never accepted Jesus Christ as my savior that I am not connected to God?"

"You are not. You must get to know God, to love God. God knows you but, accepts you as his own only through his son, Jesus Christ."

"I trust what you are saying but, I do not understand."

"Okay. I can help you begin your connection to God. God has a son and you must know his son."

"His son?"

"Yes. God's son is Jesus Christ. Jesus was born to Mary, a virgin

"I've heard about Jesus. How can a virgin bear birth? That is impossible."

"It is not impossible. If I could and I were to go into details, it's God's work and you would not understand. You could not comprehend at all. God knows no sin. That is why His spirit came here through baby Jesus to grow up and experience earthly sin, then He was to die for human sinful natures and actions. God knows no sin. Christians acknowledge and accept Jesus Christ as their savior that died after seeing sin among people, and was slain on the cross. Accepting Jesus as your Savior, being baptized, and praying to God for the forgiveness of sins has its rewards in heaven.

"Now, again, God knows no sin. He is surrounded by pure love. There is no sin whatsoever to be found near God. God knew sin was on earth among his people and he knew they could not enter heaven to praise and worship Him. He provided his son, also free of sin, to come to earth, and be amidst to see the exposure of as Satan spreading sin through people. Jesus's body died. His spirit is alive. God can not directly accept people bearing a sinful nature into his kingdom. Jesus, with His experience of association among sinful people allows His worshiper to pray and receive forgiveness of sins. They are introduced to God as "this person is now free of sin and is mine to allow acceptance into your kingdom."

"Satan hates God. He wants to devour every human, keeping you away from Jesus. The more hatred Satan can install in you, the further from Jesus he drives yoj. Satan accepters will be cast to hell with him. Satan knows you, as his, will be spend eternity in horror and he is willing to put you through that hell instead of giving in to God and allowing you to spend eternity in the loving care of God."

"So, Allow Rufus to ask you a question. Do you believe that God created our planet and the universe?"

Lonnie pauses for a few moments. "That may be. I don't see how that could happen. I have heard a different view on how creation happened. I hear opinions and believe that we did evolve from small cells to prehistoric apes and dinosaurs and gradually on to our current form over millions of years."

Rufus responds quickly. "That did not happen."

"You seem very firm in that response. How have you concluded that it did happen and what do you believe did not occur?"

"Rufus will address your questions with a "What if?" answer. As human, you should be able to comprehend the answers in your own logic."

Continuing. "I'll first address the time differences. God words that directed and influenced the bible tells you that one day in heaven may be compared to thousands of years on earth. So, at an early stage in time, if it was God's will, some creatures may have developed and changed physically but, they did not become humans. An example may be that tadpoles swam in water, then emerged from water, lost their long tails, and begin hopping around as frogs. But, which came, first the frog, or the tadpole? You know the frog lays eggs in the water and tadpoles are hatched. So, which is first the frog or tadpole?"

"I really don't know. The tadpole?"

"But, Lonnie. Does it really matter? Your God created each."

Lonnie changes the topic. "I hear that Adam and Eve were the first humans. So, you don't believe they evolved through what I call "ape men" over time to become Adam and Eve?"

"Rufus can tell you that Adam was the first humans. God breathed into his nostrils, giving Adam a soul, and gave him human life, the first human being on earth. Once Adam recognized and accepted God as the superior being over everything, God breathed into his nostrils and gave him a spirit. Animals did not and do not have a spirit. God removed a rib from Adam and made Eve."

"That makes no sense to me. How can He remove the rib from a man and use it to make a woman?

"That is beyond your comprehension. It did happen."

"Count your ribs."

"That's silly. Man has equal ribs on each side, equal to women."

"The vast majority of people have equal sets of ribs on each side. People born with certain conditions may have too many or too few ribs. So, the fact that you have equal ribs on each side is unrelated to the subject."

"Adam said, this is now bone of my bones, and flesh of my flesh: she shall be called woman because she is of man."

"Now back to emphasis on "what if?".

Remember God, and only God, knows the answer. "So, you say that God came to earth and performed all these things and returned back to heaven?"

"God has the ability to perform and task from afar. God's angels carry out much of his will"

"So, we have angels out there somewhere?"

"Spiritual angels are all around humans. God has angels that carry out his will on earth.

"Who is the devil? What is he up to?"

"The devil, Satan is a fallen angel, he and a selection of following angels tried to stand up to God, believing he could overthrow God and become the overall ruler of the universe. As a result, God cast him and his following angels out of heaven. Satan told God that he could turn a worshiper against Him and on to follow Satan. God knew better. He offered his follower, Job to Satan. In the bible Job was happy, rich, and he loved God and said, *"Job will not turn against Me. You can use Job but you must not hurt him physically."* Satan drove away his family, all his wealth, and his health. Job ended up suffering with body sores and pitiful. Job did not turn from God."

"Lonnie, what if? Rufus knows that Satan continually forges ahead to turn people away God. A simple "you don't need God". Over two hundred years ago, United States was a final reservation for Christians to relocate to from all corners of the planet. It became the foundation for God's Christian growth and expansion. It worked well. Now Satan has approached God again, "I can turn Your Christian worshipers away from You.""

"God knows the future. Satan does not know how things will turn out. God knows that Satan is incapable of stealing his worshipers. Those that do follow Satan may not have been exposed to Jesus Christ. God will fully protect those that love him and repent sins through Jesus Christ. Those non-believers that cling to lying, adulterous, gay, lesbian, and sinful ways will be with Satan in the fire pit forever.""

"Lonnie, I know things that you are not able to comprehend, or see. Satan continues against God because he still believes he can overthrow God as the Almighty."

"All this stuff is complicated. Where do you get all this information? The Bible?"

"You should believe the Bible." And Rufus expands deeper, Rufus knows."

"Now, Rufus is only able to accept and process facts. An opinion beyond factual information is based on a "what If". My "what if?" is processed by Rufus with some degree of credibility. Your question is how did Rufus conclude that God created everything. Rufus will answer that question in terms that you may easily comprehend because if I addressed the question my way, you would not understand."

Rufus continues. "Some humans have no care or belief either way. Some believe humans emerged from small cells. How did the soil and moisture that formed the earth come to be? What is the origin of the sun? The planets. Stars? How were they formed? They believe a few cells emerged and formed earth, the planets, all rotating around a bright sun?"

"You've got a point. I'm listening."

"Lonnie, humans have a book you call the Bible. In that book, time is referenced as one thousand years here on earth relate to only be one day in the location of God, called heaven. Now, that ratio of one thousand years to one day is not stated as exact, only as an example of the ratio. It may be that five thousand years is equivalent to one day. It is not a firm reference, only an example. This universe with its sun, planet, and stars that include the creation of earth was made by God in six days. Where was God during this solar system creation? Was He in another Galaxie?"

"He was where He was. That's it. He rested on the seventh day and it was sanctified. So, if each day in heaven may be equivalent to thousands, even tens of thousands of years on earth, then human perception relates differently."

"Lonnie, Rufus knows that your father died at 6:07 p.m. on June 11th 23 years ago. Now, assume that you may die in another 35 years from now. Considering the time difference, you may join him in God's time within less than one minute after his arrival in heaven, even though it has been over 43 years on earth. Make sense?"

Lonnie says. "This is some pretty deep stuff. I'm going to need some time and attempt to understand what you are saying. Why Should I believe in the Bible? It was written by men and, it repeats itself throughout."

Rufus responds with an example. "You say the bible repeats itself. Different people experience and repeat the biblical stories."

"What if you are in Atlanta, Georgia and witnessed a building collapsing at one pm. A human from Seattle, Washington is visiting and sees the same event at the same time you see it. The next day you report details of the collapse to the news media in your hometown. The other human from Seattle shares what he saw and experienced with the news in Seattle. Both stories tell of the same event. You would have no reason to doubt the reporting by two different people that did not know each other and both stories are near identical."

"Do you understand?"

"I guess so."

"In your bible the same event is also witnessed and written by persons that recorded their witnessing in their separate books contained within the bible."

"An example is when Jesus walked on water. Three men tell of the feat, each in three separate writings. Each of the three tells of the same event, in a different writing.

"That makes sense. However, books in the bible were written by man, not God. Am I right?"

"You are right in that your bible was written by man under his penmanship. However, the spirit of God influenced and guided each man to write the entire message in each book, word for word, with no variance whatsoever."

"What is a soul? a spirit? Aren't they about the same?"

"Aha! Man has a soul. Man may not yet possess the spirit of God."

"I don't understand."

"Man's soul possesses his lifelong experiences. The spirit is human relationship and connection to your savior, Jesus's Christ. Acquiring a spirit is a step-by-step process. You have sinned throughout life and if you fully understand and accept Jesus Christ as your redeemer before witnesses and have prayed forgiveness or your sins, then Jesus recognizes and rewards you in that your past sins no longer exist. God knows no sin. God has never been exposed to any sin. So, Jesus Christ was exposed to the sins of this earth and He is human's only way to stand before God.

"The soul bears your earthly experiences and your spirit connection to Jesus is you only way to heaven."

"Under God's design of mankind, the spirit is within a person's mind and heart."

"Do we look like God?"

"No human eyes have ever seen God. God tells us that he created man in his image. That image may or may not be exactly as we expect."

"Where is God and how did he make earth?"

"Rufus will answer with a "what if" while referencing elementary studies of Nuclear Physics. We'll compare the make-up of this universe to a small atom. The nucleus, centrally located consists of protons and neutrons. Then electrons rotate around the nucleus. Visualize the sun as a huge nucleus and electrons, known by humans as planets rotating around the nucleus or sun. The combination of electrons, neutrons, protons in nuclear physics is known as an atom."

"Do you have questions?"

"Go ahead. At this point I don't know enough to ask a question. Go on."

"Allow me to use pens to illustrate for you. I will use a black, green, yellow, and red pen.

"Now, Rufus will very quickly sketch a version of an atom."

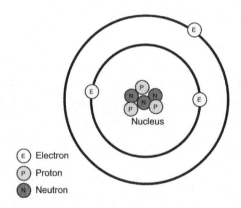

"And you know that? Wow!"

"Okay, stay with Rufus. My artwork is for illustrative purposes only. Look at my drawing as you are peering into our universe from way above. In the center is the nucleus or sun. Rotating around the nucleus or sun are electrons. Visualize the electrons as planets. Now, do you see our earth rotating around the sun? Now, visualize many other solar systems or universes tightly nudging our system on all sides."

"Make sense to you, Lonnie?"

"It's far above my head but, it is beginning to sink in. Where is heaven and God?"

"Ask him when you get there."

"But, how do you know all this stuff? And, are you certain that it's for real?"

"I believe what I am telling you. You should pay attention to everything I am saying."

"I'm still not sure that there is a God, that God offers a forever life to me."

"Lonnie, I'll ask you one important question. What have you got to lose? What if, as you tend to believe, you die and never experience anything afterwards. You decompose just like a vegetable and no longer exist in any form?"

"Or, you do live here on earth, day by day, never accepting Christ, and you die, joining Satan in a pit of fire forever and among horrible people. You then want Jesus Christ to accept you but, it's too late. He does not recognize you?"

"Or, you decide to start by studying the bible, pursuing religion, getting to know Christ, and learn to love God and, as a result, you live forever as a new being with no suffering, only a surrounding of love?"

"Please listen carefully. Earlier, over the last few days and meetings, some of you have heard me offer a promise as to how you can successfully deal with and overcome all the frustrations in America and across the planet. Your worries about communism, money, war, and even a man-made electromagnetic pulse that disables all electronics. You will not have phone services, no heat and air, no television, no computers, no access to cash or, even groceries. Automobiles will not run. You may be stranded on the side of a highway many miles from home and your loved ones. Airplanes fall from the air due to their lack of electronic control."

"You may be asking, how severe is the threat of a EMP attack?"

"China now has a network of satellites, high-speed missiles, and super-EMP... report on China's ability to conduct an Electromagnetic Pulse attack on the United States.... attack that could produce a deadly blackout to the entire country. Russia, Iran, and North Korea are also in mix."

"And, here's Rufus trying to convince you there of a solution?"

"Open up your mind for a spell. Look at the total scene. Accept the fact that you are going to be alive, naturally for one hundred years. Pre-mature death may take you out within the hour. It can happen. You have heard there is a better place that your spirit can be welcomed into. All you need to do is accept God. Accept his son, Jesus Christ as your savior. Pray to God, include and pray to God through his Son Jesus Christ. Ask Jesus Christ to forgive you of your sins. That's all. Quite simple, is it not? What have you got to lose?"

"If you still lean toward the assumption that when you die, you just rot away and no longer exist anywhere, what if I'm right? What if the bible that was written thousands of years ago under the direct influence of the Almighty God is right, and has remained as it is through the test of time? So, for you to consider turning to God and learning more, what have you got to lose?"

"Better yet, what have you got to gain? Rufus knows of Christians that will vow that after they turned to the Lord, their whole life began to become wholesome. They were happier than they had ever dreamed. You have the opportunity to step in a new life that will even impress yourself. If it impresses you, God begins to share his spirit with you and you'll feel his presence. Amazing isn't it?"

"One more time, what have you got to lose?"

Pearsall walks up to the stage center. "Rufus, thank you so very much. The information you have shared is so important to all of us."

The audience stands as they clap for Rufus.

Carl comes forward as Rufus steps back. "Rufus and I thank you for attending this session. We thank the staff and their diligent work in setting up the facility for this meeting. May God Bless each of you."

"Good afternoon."

CHAPTER 13

The room begins to evacuate and guests walk by Carl as he stands near the exit. Carl is making it a point to show appreciation to each guest as they leave. Rufus remains near the speaker platform and is surrounded by a few guests that seem to be very curious and desiring a one-on-one with the speaker. Four men, Butch Hallotham, Lanny Whispo, Mark stoworne, and Jimmy Miccossuke are scattered about the room and make their way toward Butch, shaking hands with each other as if they just met.

Butch tells the other three. "I want to meet Carl. Jimmy, do you want to walk over there with me?"

"You bet."

Jimmy follows Butch over to meet Carl. Butch reaches out to shake the hand of Carl as he offers a thanks for all the arrangements. "That Rufus is something else. It's absolutely amazing, the broad range of intelligence he possesses."

"Well, thank you sir."

Lanny approaches Rufus first. "Rufus, my name is Lanny Whispoo. I was anxious to meet you today. I have a question. Do you sleep at all? What do you do in your spare time?"

"I never sleep. There is no need to rest or sleep. I do not tire out."

Rufus detects slight nervousness in Mark. He reaches out to Mark's wrist, pulling him slightly closer, "Mark, Rufus likes you. I hope you like Rufus."

"Oh yes. Yes, I do like you."

Lanny takes over with the conversation again. "Rufus, I must go now. I have another engagement and, it's one that I don't want to be late to arrive. I am thrilled to have engaged with you today."

"Mark, do you want to stay?"

"No, I'll walk out with you."

Lanny and Mark walked out of the room, then were followed by Butch and Jimmy. Carl picked up on the relationship of the four as close friends. Rufus paid close attention to their foursome exit. Combining that with the nervous attitude by Mark caused some speculation of something strange. But Rufus retained no real concern.

As they get ready to leave the building, Rufus noticed an awkward electronical sensation about his head. It was a brief buzzing sensation. However, he has no concern. His electronics are designed to self-analyzation and self-repair when and if needed.

Rufus and Carl walk alongside each other toward the parking lot and their vehicle.

"Rufus, the head count in that Conference hall today was six hundred forty-one. John told me that they have had very few events over the ten-year life of the facility that drew many people. You have suddenly become not only a local celebrity but, you're gaining regional and probably national recognition. You are truly a hero. Amazing."

No response from Rufus.

As they leave for home, Carl wants to go to his store. The drive is about fifteen minutes from the Conference Center to his jewelry store. Traffic is light. Carl notices that Rufus is very quiet.

"Rufus, you're not saying much. What's up? What's on your mind?"

"Oh, nothing, really. I'm probably just a little moody."

"Moody? Rufus, you haven't had a moody moment since we adopted you. Come on now. What's going on?"

"I just want to take it easy for a while, to rest."

Carl parks in front of the store. "Want to come in with me?"

"Not this time."

Carl is concerned. Rufus has never acted like this. He decides to leave Rufus behind and briefly visit the store, about ten minutes at the most.

Rufus remains in the car. At the moment, he is staring at the car floor as he attempts to hold his thoughts. He needs to contact the plant yet he can't hold any thought long enough to pull up the contact information. He knows something unusual and concerning is going on. His thoughts keep jumping around, holding any attempted concentrated thought only about two seconds.

Carl is returning to the car now. He notices Rufus's concerns as he approaches. Opening the driver door, Carl goes to his knees and rests both arms on the driver seat. "Rufus. Rufus, my friend. Tell me what's going on. Let me help you. Come on. Please."

No response. Rufus makes brief eye contact with Carl, then he turns away.

Now, Carl is nearing panic. "Something is wrong with Rufus."

He pulls out his phone and dials the phone number to LRC, the robot headquarters.

"LRC. This is Beatrice. How may I direct your call.?"

"Beatrice I am Carl, owner of Rufus. This is an emergency. I must speak to service at once. Please."

"Yes. You are being connected as we speak."

Instead of transferring the call within the LRC facility, she sends the call to Hugh Barton at another location.

"Hello, this is Hugh Barton. What is the emergency?"

"Hugh, it seems that Rufus is unable to concentrate, something is wrong."

"What has he been doing within the last hour?"

"He concluded a meeting with over six hundred people in the audience and then, we drove to my store. He has had almost nothing to say since that meeting."

"Carl, did he have one-on-one contact with two or more individuals before you left for your store?"

"Yes. He talked to a couple of men. In fact, there were four of guys that I believe were together because they left together."

"Carl! Look around your area now! Scan the area closely. Do you see one or more of those men nearby, sitting in car, standing around, or anywhere in your line of sight?"

"No. Well, there is a black SUV with dark windows parked across the street, facing this way. Their running lights are on. I can't see inside that vehicle from here."

"Carl, you have a problem. Is Rufus still in your car?"

"Yes."

"Okay. Go to NW General Aviation immediately. Drive there quickly while trying to lose any vehicle that may be following you. That SUV will probably follow. We'll have a Gulfstream G650ER waiting for you to board. You and Rufus will be here in about forty minutes. We'll have a limo waiting for you. You and Rufus must get here as quick as possible. If you need assistance getting Rufus on the plane, the pilot will help you. Hurry!"

"Okay. I'm on my way! I'll go by my house and pick up Judy and we'll be on our way. Thank you."

"No! Carl, you must go directly to the airport. Do not go home. Go to NW General Aviation as quickly as you can get there. Do you understand?"

"Okay. I'll update Judy on my way to the plane."

"If you detect others following you to the airport, call me back. We can have their vehicle detained before the airstrip gate."

"Okay. I'm on my way."

Carl pulls his car out and heads east bound. In the mirror, as somewhat anticipated, he sees that SUV become part of the east bound traffic. He continues while being very observant of traffic behind him.

"Aha, Carl whispers to himself. That SUV had to stop for the traffic light behind me. I now have an advantage and will stay ahead of them. Just to be safe, I'll turn off the circle and head down highway 27 alternate."

He continues to watch for that SUV and believes he out-witted them. There is now a gold color sedan behind, but of no concern to Carl.

Carl looks at the dash and time of day displayed. "I'm making good travel time."

His cell phone rings and he sees a text from Hugh at RNC. The message provides an airport gate opener code of 828337.

Turning off the highway and back on the circle that leads to the airport, he is still observant of vehicles behind his.

"That gold sedan is probably going to the regional airport and, I'll turn just before that and out to NW General Aviation."

He turns onto the entrance road to NW. That gold sedan has sped up and is now immediately behind Carl and Rufus.

"Uh oh. I've got a problem! That car is now trying to pull alongside me on this narrow road. That driver is nuts! This is a one lane entrance road and he's trying to pass me? No! He wants to force me off the road!"

Carl is now driving defensively as he swerves to keep that car behind him. As he enters the parking lot area, he speeds up toward the security gate. The other car is close behind him, fol-lowing as closely as five feet.

Approaching the gate, Carl quickly rolls down his window and reaches out to the pad. He hears car doors and movement behind him as he enters the code and rolls up the widow. Two strange men quickly appear at both front car doors, hollering orders for him to unlock the doors and step outside the car.

Now, Carl is shaking as he wants the gate to hastily open. "Why is that gate so slow", he thinks.

The gate is now about two thirds open. He turns the steering wheel to the left and accelerates full speed forward, tapping the partially opened gate with the right front edge of his car. Still full throttled, he races toward a Gulfstream parked as if ready for passengers. The jets are running as if it is ready to taxi out to the runway and go airborne. As he reaches the plane and slams on the brakes, he calls out to Rufus.

"Rufus! Rufus! We gotta' go man. Let's go!"

Rufus understands some of the orders and proceeds to open his door. Carl motions to the pilot to help get Rufus on the plane. A sense of urgency is now obvious and the pilot runs the few steps to help.

At the gate, by the time the strangers returned to their car, the gate had automatically closed almost half way. Instead of ramming the gate they surrendered their efforts and sat watching Carl and Rufus board the plane.

Rufus becomes more alert as he recognizes that something may be harmful to Carl. He responds by hurriedly advancing toward the plane entrance ramp.

All three are now on board. The pilot is raising the ramp as he prepares for taxi to runway twenty-one.

The pilot introduces himself. "You are Carl? And I believe that is Rufus? My name is Brad Microne. I'll get us outta' here in a jiffy", he says as he throttles the Gulfstream away from the building. He has just been cleared for takeoff.

"Oh heck! What about my car? It's still sitting there."

Brad tells Carl, "They have already arranged for your car to be secured and awaiting your return. It will be okay."

The Gulfstream climbs rapidly to twenty-nine thousand feet and levels off. Within a few short minutes, the plane is on its initial approach to the destination air strip. "That is faster than fast!" Carl remarks.

Rufus remains very quiet and semi-responsive as the plane's landing gear is lowered and Carl can see the RNC facility off in the distance. "All that has gone on over the last hour is scary.", he reasons.

On the ground, Brad pulls the plane up near a stretch limousine that is waiting to drive Carl and Rufus to RNC. Rufus acknowledges he is expected to follow Carl off the plane and to the waiting limo.

It's only a six-minute drive to a warehouse near the airport.

Carl thinks, "I didn't realize that RNC had other buildings scattered about the town. He sees a sign on the building reading "RNC Scientific Division". He steps out of the limousine and to one side as three young men grab Rufus. Carl follows them to the building and on inside. "Carl, I'm Hugh. We talked earlier."

"Yes, I remember. What's wrong with Rufus? Do you know?"

"We do. RNC went in to an emergency mode immediately following your contact with us. We'll be able to disengage the altered circuitry, bringing Rufus back to normal."

"Whew. Thank you, thank you! I believe I would have given my life for Rufus. I really do!"

"Carl, why don't you sit down in the lobby, relax, and have a cup of coffee. My team is already working with Rufus and he'll be returned to you within half an hour. He'll be normal again. And, we're installing a guard to avoid such as this going forward. Isn't that great?"

"It is. I'm glad you all are on top of this problem."

"Oh crap, I didn't call Judy!"

On his phone, Carl pressed a fast call code to Judy.

"Hello."

"Judy, what's my darling wife doing at the moment?"

"Oh, I just got off the phone on a long conversation with my niece. And you?"

"At the moment I'm relaxing at the RNC offices."

"No way! That's impossible."

"Not really. RNC flew Rufus and me up here. They wanted to update some circuitry on Rufus. So, here we are."

"You flew there?"

"We did. It probably took less than thirty minutes on a small, very fast jet. I anticipate that we'll be back at the airport within the next hour or so. I'll call you as we take off from here."

"Oh my gosh! Please keep me abreast as to what is going on. Okay?"

"Absolutely, I'll do that."

Sipping on his coffee, Carl thinks back over the last couple of hours. All the strange and scary developments now seem fictional.

"How did all this happen so quickly?"

He hears footsteps coming toward him. "Okay. Carl, Rufus is back and better than normal. He is coming this way."

"Great!"

Rufus! Wow! Look at you! You're back! Let's go home!"

As they approach the limo, "Rufus knows you, Carl."

"That's different." Carl thinks. "Rufus's normal greeting is "Rufus likes you."

"Rufus, within less than an hour we'll be home. We've had a whirlwind afternoon, haven't we?"

"Yes, we have."

The limousine drives away as it drives Rufus and Carl back toward the waiting Gulfstream.

Back at the warehouse, Hugh is busy giving orders to his group. "Okay guys, you know the drill. Get those signs down. Pull out all the technical equipment and load it back in the rental van. We've got less than one hour to get this place back to its normal state and, get outta' here."

Hugh steps aside to a quiet area and dials his associate in New York. "Geraldo, our mission is accomplished. The agents back in Rufus's town caused panic in Carl and forced him to the waiting plane that brought them to us. We have now successfully installed the RJ607 chip in that robot for connection to your system."

"Congratulations, Hugh. Job well planned and carried out by you boys. That robot is now under our control and will share its United States secrets with us, on demand. Your earned ten-million-dollar bonus has just completed its transfer to your foreign bank account. Your confirmation code for the funds transfer is Qti50j13mBv84-0015. Write that confirmation down while we speak. I'll slowly repeat that code for you. It is Q t I 5 0 j 1 3 m B v 8 4 – 0 0 1 5. Again, Congratulations. This concludes our conversation and interaction from this time forward. Good bye."

ABOUT THE AUTHOR

 J. Andy Welch is said to possess an abnormal sense of creativity and imagination. His creative ability first came to light with an invention several years ago. He identified the need for a computerized storage, dispensing, and refiling system. Without the initial aid of pen and paper, he configured the basic system in his mind. Following design and prototyping, the patented system stood out as being one-of-a-kind, worldwide.

That "no notes" mentality has folded forward as his publications continue to be written with no outline or notes to follow. Welch is seated at his laptop and begins to write. As he writes, he has no extended foresight as to what will happen next in the composition. His writing develops into a flow of events, as if he followed a perfect outline. Welch actually believes an outline could distort the natural flow.

"I see Rufus as a friend. He is the product of an active imagination, combined with months of extensive research and ambitious drive. "Rufus I" is a terrific read. And, I believe you will enjoy viewing him as your friend." J.A.W.

Made in the USA
Columbia, SC
13 May 2021